Angels in disguise . . .

"Look out!" Elizabeth yelled as Allison Meyer knocked over a doll carriage filled with building blocks.

Evie, holding a struggling Yuky, said, "I think there's something in the water today. These kids are all acting crazy!"

Crazy was putting it mildly, I thought. I was sure glad I didn't have to deal with those other kids. Ellie was so good. Then again, maybe Ellie was good because of the way I treated her. If Ellie had been acting fresh, I would have talked to her instead of yelling at her the way Ellen yelled at Arthur Foo or Jessica yelled at Oliver. I think Ellie knew that. It was a matter of mutual respect.

"Ellie isn't acting crazy," I told Evie. "It's just a matter of knowing how to handle children."

Ellen rolled her eyes. "Get real, Lila," she said. "It's just a matter of giving them time out for about a month!" She glowered at Arthur.

I shrugged. "Well, it seems to me that some of us are able to handle children and some of us aren't," I said, smiling down at Ellie. Maybe it was silly, but I wanted to show the Unicorns that I knew how to take care of children. You didn't have to have a mom around to know how to do that.

THE UNICORN CLUB™

LILA'S LITTLE SISTER

Written by
Alice Nicole Johansson

Created by
FRANCINE PASCAL

BANTAM BOOKS
NEW YORK•TORONTO•LONDON•SYDNEY•AUCKLAND

RL 4, 008-012

LILA'S LITTLE SISTER
A Bantam Book / April 1994

Sweet Valley High® *and The Unicorn Club*™
are trademarks of Francine Pascal

Conceived by Francine Pascal

Produced by Daniel Weiss Associates, Inc.
33 West 17th Street
New York, NY 10011

Cover art by James Mathewuse

ISBN: 0-553-48214-9

Published simultaneously in the United States and Canada

Bantam Books are published by Bantam Books, a division of Bantam
Doubleday Dell Publishing Group, Inc. Its trademark, consisting of the
words "Bantam Books" and the portrayal of a rooster, is Registered in U.S.
Patent and Trademark Office and in other countries. Marca Registrada.
Bantam Books, 1540 Broadway, New York, New York 10036.

PRINTED IN THE UNITED STATES OF AMERICA

OPM   0 9 8 7 6 5 4 3 2 1

112730

To Nicole Pascal Johansson

One

"I wonder who else is here?" I said to Mrs. McMillan as we left the limousine and headed toward the lobby of my dad's company, Fowler Enterprises.

It was Friday, and the girls of Sweet Valley Middle School were participating in a bring-your-daughter-to-work day. It was designed to boost the girls' morale and self-esteem. The way the day worked was mothers were encouraged to bring their daughters to work to show them what women are doing in the workplace. My mom and I aren't exactly close these days—she lives in Europe—but I wasn't about to pass up the chance to miss a day of school. So I asked Mrs. McMillan if she would be my "mom" for the day.

"I hope *someone* I know is here," I said. I hated to be the first one to arrive somewhere.

"I guess we'll soon find out," Mrs. McMillan said as we walked into the lobby.

Did we ever! Mothers and daughters practically filled the huge domed lobby of Fowler Enterprises. I guess I shouldn't have been surprised. A lot of people in Sweet Valley work for my dad. Including Mrs. McMillan. But that's not the only reason I asked her to be my "mom." Mrs. McMillan is also a friend. And her daughter, Ellie, and I have a very special relationship. Ellie's like the little sister I never had.

I stood on tiptoe to look around the lobby. Was anyone I knew there? Then through the crowd I saw Jessica and Elizabeth Wakefield. They were standing with their mom near one of the big potted palms that flanked the brass doors to the main offices of Fowler Enterprises, and they were waiting for the doors to open. Their mom is an interior decorator, and she was redecorating some of the conference rooms.

"The Wakefields are here!" I said to Mrs. McMillan, pointing across the bustling lobby. "See them?"

"How could I miss them?" Mrs. McMillan said with a smile. "It's like having double vision."

I grinned. You see, Jessica and Elizabeth are identical twins. Both have sun-streaked blond hair and these fabulous blue-green eyes, and both are in the Unicorn Club. Jessica's been in the club for as long as I have, but Elizabeth just joined this year.

Elizabeth's the brainy type. She used to believe that all the Unicorns thought about were boys and clothes. Last year, I guess that was true. But we've changed. I don't know, I guess we're more serious now. Don't get me wrong, we still like to have fun, but . . . well, maybe we just grew up a bit.

After Elizabeth saw the work we did at the day-care center, she changed her mind. She and her friend Maria Slater even helped change the principal's mind about disbanding the Unicorn Club after Jessica and I stole his toupee during a dare war to see which one of us would be the new president. So of course we asked the two of them to join the club.

Pretty confusing, huh? In case you've forgotten some of the history of the Unicorn Club, let me refresh your memory. I, Lila Fowler, am one of its original members. I'm in the seventh grade now, but I've been in the club since the sixth grade. My cousin, Janet Howell, used to be the president, but she went on to Sweet Valley High this year, so we had to elect a new president.

Naturally, I was in the running. So was Jessica Wakefield, since she's also one of the club's original members. But Jessica and I ended up forfeiting the position to Mandy Miller. Mandy has tons of common sense, and she sees the best in all of us. She helps us to see it, too. She doesn't have a lot of money or anything, but she has the coolest clothes. She buys them mostly at thrift shops. I would probably never dress that way, but I really like Mandy's funky chic look.

Not that you have to be a great dresser to be a Unicorn. Things like clothes and hair aren't as important to us as they used to be. Oh, we still like to look cool, and purple is still our official color. But we've discovered that it's what's inside a person that counts, and that the best clubs bring out the best in their members. Anyhow, that's what Mandy always says. So far this year, the Unicorn Club has done some pretty excellent things for Sweet Valley, if I do say so myself.

Take Ellie and Mrs. McMillan, for instance. I got to know them when the Unicorns had to work at the Sweet Valley Child Care Center. It was our punishment after we stole the principal's toupee and did a few other crummy things. Even though it was only Jessica and I who swiped the toupee, the Unicorns are a one-for-all-and-all-for-one club. If something is done in the club's name, we all take responsibility for it. So we all shared the punishment.

Getting caught with Mr. Clark's toupee was the final straw in a whole series of events, like painting a purple stripe down the lockers of Sweet Valley Middle School. As you can imagine, I wasn't happy when we were sentenced to working with a bunch of noisy, messy kids for thirty whole hours.

Then this adorable little four-year-old, Ellie, just decided I was her friend. She thinks I'm really pretty, and I think she's just as cute as I was at her age. She's really tiny, and she has these gorgeous dark curls and big dark eyes.

But what I love most about Ellie is that she's so sweet! Of course, all of the kids are special—that's why we decided to keep volunteering at the day-care center even after our sentence was up. But Ellie will always be my favorite. I even asked my father to find Mrs. McMillan a job at Fowler Enterprises. Mrs. McMillan had to put Ellie in foster care for a while because she was unemployed and couldn't afford to take care of her. It sounded so awful to have to worry about where your next meal was coming from and whether you could pay the rent.

I scanned the crowd again. How was I going to make it over to Jessica and Elizabeth through this mob? Exasperated, I yelled, "Jessica! Elizabeth!" across the lobby.

"Lila!" Jessica called back. She looked really happy to see me, which made me feel good. Jessica is best friends with Elizabeth—after all, they are twins—but Jessica and I are also best friends.

Jessica, Elizabeth, and Mrs. Wakefield managed to squeeze their way through the crowd to join us. Then Mrs. McMillan and Mrs. Wakefield went off to the refreshment table to get some coffee. While they were gone, Elizabeth, Jessica, and I moved to the sidelines to talk. Just then, Mary Wallace and Ellen Riteman came over with their mothers. Mary and Ellen are both Unicorns, too. Mary's mom does market research for Dad's company, and Ellen's mom works for an accounting firm that was in the middle of going over Fowler Enterprises' books.

"How's it goin'?" Mary said, as she made her way over to us. Mary's in the eighth grade. She's got long blond hair and gray eyes and she's perfect for looking great in almost any kind of clothes—tall and slim—although she dresses a little preppier than I like. You know, lots of khakis and oxford shirts.

"Isn't this great?" she said. "Not only do we get out of school, but my mom's taking me to lunch at the Curly Cucumber."

"The Curly Cucumber is a pretty good restaurant, but I think it's a little overrated," I said. "Maison Jacques is much better. They make the most fabulous lobster bisque."

"How can you like that stuff?" Mary shivered as if she thought it was disgusting. "And anyway, who wants to spend a thousand dollars for lunch?" she said.

Mrs. Wallace looked thoughtful. "Actually, Mary, I don't think lunch for the two of us at Maison Jacques would cost quite that much," she said.

Mrs. Wallace tended to take everything literally.

Ellen giggled.

"Don't giggle," her mother admonished, shaking a finger at her. "It's not ladylike."

Ellen waited until her mother turned back toward Mrs. Wallace and started talking. Then she began shaking her finger at us and making a stern face just like her mother's. Mrs. Riteman can be pretty obnoxious. She thinks she knows everything, and she's always pushing Ellen to do stuff she doesn't want to do. I don't know how Ellen stands it. We all had to cover our mouths to keep from laughing out loud.

I scanned the rest of the crowd. Evie Kim, the

sixth-grade member of the Unicorns, wasn't there. Evie's Korean-American and a really talented violinist. She lives with her grandmother, an ex–movie star who owns a thrift shop called The Attic. Evie was probably at the shop today. Maria's mom doesn't have a job outside the house, so I wasn't sure where she was. And Mandy's mom is a seamstress, so I figured Mandy was working with her today.

"So," Jessica said to keep us from cracking up again when Ellen started another mom mimic, this time crossing her eyes, "what's everybody wearing to the Seventh Heaven Weekend dance?"

Ellen uncrossed her eyes and twirled around. She was wearing purple leggings and an oversize purple-and-red-striped tunic. "My mom and I went to Kendall's yesterday," she said to Jessica, "and we found this to-die-for gold-and-blue off-the-shoulder party dress with a flounce skirt."

"My mom and I were at Kendall's yesterday, too," Mary said. "They were having a great sale. I found an incredible pair of jeans."

"I found a great outfit, too," Jessica said. She made a face. "But my mom said it was too old for me."

"It *was* too old for you, Jessica," Elizabeth said. She turned to the rest of us. "It was red, with a low, scoop back and a lace bodice."

Jessica sighed. "It was gorgeous. I wish I could have talked Mom into buying it."

I laughed along with everybody else, but I felt

a kind of tug inside. I wondered what it would
be like to have a mother to shop with.

Then I tossed my hair over my shoulders. It
wasn't such a big deal. When I have to buy a party
dress, I just call the personal shopper at Mes Amis.
She's trained to find the right dress for you.
Besides, the Seventh Heaven Weekend, which is an
annual event exclusively for seventh graders, includes not only the Friday-night dance but also a
field day on Saturday (where there are things like
relay races and watermelon-eating contests). And
on Sunday night there's a potluck supper. My dad
promised to take me to the potluck supper, and
that's more important than any party dress.

"What's everybody bringing to the Sunday-
night supper?" I asked, to change the subject.

"Mom's going to help Elizabeth and me make her
famous shepherd's pie," Jessica said. "It's awesome!"

"I'm trying to decide between broccoli-chicken
bake and pot roast," said Ellen.

"You actually know how to make pot roast?"
Elizabeth said.

Ellen nodded. "I happen to like pot roast," she
said. "So my mom taught me how to make it."

"What are you bringing, Lila?" Elizabeth asked.

Actually, I'd been planning to bring one of the
duck and tortilla casseroles they sell frozen at Tilly's.
What could be better than one of Tilly's casseroles?
We always keep some of them in our freezer at
home. I figured that on the big night my dad and I

could just pop one into the microwave and go. I felt a little funny mentioning that now. But that was mostly because I didn't want everyone to feel bad that they weren't bringing anything nearly as good.

Luckily, Mrs. Wakefield and Mrs. McMillan returned just then and interrupted our conversation. "So what have you girls been talking about?" Mrs. Wakefield asked, smoothing Jessica's loose blond hair and then reaching over to straighten the purple scarf tying Elizabeth's ponytail. I felt a twinge of jealousy seeing Mrs. Wakefield do that. Mrs. Pervis often picked a piece of lint off one of my sweaters, or a loose hair off my shoulder, but somehow it just wasn't the same.

"We've been talking about the Seventh Heaven Weekend," Jessica told Mrs. Wakefield.

Mrs. Riteman straightened the hem of Ellen's tunic.

"Ellen, Ellen, Ellen," she said, "you do manage to muss your clothes in no time flat."

Mary, Elizabeth, and Jessica managed to hold their giggles in, but I couldn't help myself. Mrs. Riteman was such a fussbudget. I burst out laughing.

Mrs. Riteman stood up and glared at me. "I don't see what's so funny about neatness, Lila," she said.

Mrs. McMillan jumped to my rescue. I could tell she thought Mrs. Riteman was abnormally fussy, too. "I'm sure Lila didn't mean anything by it," she said.

Mrs. Riteman shook her head. "Maybe not," she said. "I suppose it's her upbringing. It must be awfully hard for Mr. Fowler to raise a girl like Lila without a mother."

Mrs. McMillan looked totally embarrassed. She didn't seem to know what to say. Mrs. Riteman was being so obnoxious. Like I'm some kind of spoiled brat who needs to be straightened out, or my dad isn't a good parent!

Well, I wasn't about to let her get away with that. I turned to Mrs. McMillan. "You know," I said, loud enough for everyone to hear, "I think this mother/daughter day is a great idea, but really, how difficult can being a mother be? I mean, if it was that hard, wouldn't moms be, like, paid or something? My dad—who, by the way, is a wonderful father—says that everybody likes to make what they do seem more important than it really is. Mothers are probably like that, too."

"I don't know about that, Lila," Mrs. Wallace said. She looked at Mrs. Wakefield and smiled.

I looked around. Mrs. Riteman was tapping her foot impatiently, as if she couldn't wait for someone to explain to me how naive I was. Mrs. McMillan just shook her head slightly. Even the Unicorns were smiling, like there was some joke in the air that I wasn't getting.

"I'm serious," I said, feeling my cheeks grow red. "How hard can mothering be?"

"When you have to stay up for three nights in a row with a colicky baby, you'll understand," Mrs. McMillan said.

Mrs. Wakefield nodded. "Babies take a lot of care and patience," she said. "But I think the most difficult part of being a mother is sticking to your guns, being consistent. A mother has to mean what she says, whether it's something a child wants to hear or not. She has to stand by her word and keep her promises, be someone her kids can trust." She sighed. "It's not always easy," she added.

I didn't know what to say. Luckily, the doors to Fowler Enterprises opened, and the employees and their daughters began to file in to start their day.

"Come on," Mrs. McMillan said. Taking me by the hand, she led me to her office.

"Well, what do you think?" she asked when we came to a small office with a brass nameplate that said LINDA MCMILLAN next to the entrance.

I looked around. It was a big-enough space, I guess, although I would have preferred it if the walls were a nice warm color like rose or ivory. Instead they were flat white. Which, I guess, went best with the modern, airy decor. There were pictures of Ellie all over a corkboard behind Mrs. McMillan's desk. On top of the desk were several large computers.

"This is the computer system I'm working on," Mrs. McMillan said proudly. "It will link Fowler Enterprises offices from coast to coast."

"How?" I asked. As you might have figured, I'm not exactly a computer whiz.

"By letting our computers talk to each other," she said.

"Talk to each other?"

Mrs. McMillan smiled. "*Communicate* is probably a better word," she said. "By using what's called a modem, computers can communicate with each other over the phone lines. Do you want to see how it works? We've got parts of the system in place already."

"Um, sure," I said. I wasn't really interested, but I couldn't exactly say that. Mrs. McMillan definitely had the most boring job in the whole universe.

"I have to send a document to our New York office," Mrs. McMillan said. "Here, let me show you."

She typed some stuff into the computer, and a sound like a telephone being dialed came out of the computer. Then there was this high-pitched beep, and Mrs. McMillan grinned.

"Done!" she said.

"I guess it beats sending it by mail."

We spent the rest of the morning working on the computers. After a few hours, I actually began to like working on the computers. Don't tell Jessica, though. She'd never let me hear the end of it.

"So what do you think of our computer network?" Mrs. McMillan asked, after sending another document to New York using the modem. It was just after noon.

"It's great," I said. "But do computers ever get a break? I'm starving," I said.

Mrs. McMillan laughed. "Me, too," she said. "How does the company cafeteria sound?"

It sounded boring, but I knew Mrs. McMillan didn't have a lot of money, and the cafeteria was inexpensive. "Anyplace I can get a salad is fine," I told her.

"The cafeteria has an entire salad bar," she said, picking up her purse.

"Great!" I said.

We stepped out of Mrs. McMillan's office and started toward the elevators. We hadn't walked three feet when a man came flying around the corner. Before I could even say, "Look out!" he and Mrs. McMillan bumped their heads together with a tremendous crack!

Books and papers and the contents of Mrs. McMillan's purse flew in every direction.

"I'm so sorry," the man said, picking up Mrs. McMillan's wallet and handing it to her.

"It was my fault. I wasn't looking where I was going," Mrs. McMillan countered, picking up the man's papers and books. They stood at the same time, their hands extended to return the other's property.

Their eyes met and held. They just stood there staring at each other. I've seen enough movies to know what was going on. I knew right away that the books, the purse, and the crack on the head were totally out of the picture now. Mrs. McMillan and the man weren't aware of anything but each other.

I couldn't help smiling. I may not know a lot, but I was certain of one thing: this was an obvious case of love at first sight.

Two

"Gerard Stillman!" Mrs. McMillan said. "It's been years!"

I guess I should have said love at second sight. Apparently, Mrs. McMillan knew this guy.

"How are you, Linda?" Mr. Stillman asked.

He was kind of cute, I thought. He had dark-brown hair and hazel eyes, and a smile that lifted on one side.

"I'm fine . . . um, great," Mrs. McMillan said, still a little dazed. Then, remembering that I was there, she said, "Oh, excuse me. Lila Fowler, this is Gerard Stillman. We used to date years ago."

So that explained it. "Nice to meet you, Mr. Stillman," I said. Mr. Stillman smiled that cute, crooked smile again.

"Nice to meet you, too, Lila," he said.

"Lila's here for a bring-your-daughter-to-work day. It's sponsored by her school. I'm filling in as Lila's mom." She paused for a moment. "So what brings you to this neck of the woods, Gerard?"

"Actually," Mr. Stillman said, "I work here."

Mrs. McMillan looked a little confused. "But then, why haven't I seen you around before?"

"I just transferred to the Sweet Valley office last week," Mr. Stillman said.

"Oh," Mrs. McMillan said.

Mr. Stillman nodded. He seemed unable to take his eyes off Mrs. McMillan. He laughed self-consciously. "I was just going to get some lunch in the cafeteria," he said at last. "Would you ladies care to join me?"

Mrs. McMillan glanced at me.

"Sure," I said.

"Then that would be lovely," Mrs. McMillan said.

The cafeteria is on the top floor of Fowler Enterprises. Mrs. McMillan and Mr. Stillman bought tuna sandwiches and sodas. I had a glass of mineral water and a salad. We sat by a window overlooking the city. It was a great view, but Mr. Stillman and Mrs. McMillan didn't stop looking at each other long enough to notice.

"So what brought you to Sweet Valley?" Mr. Stillman asked Mrs. McMillan.

Mrs. McMillan took a sip of her soda. "After my

husband and I were divorced," she said, "I moved to Sweet Valley to raise my little girl. It seemed like a better place to raise a child than Los Angeles. You know, quieter." She smiled at me. "I wouldn't have been able to stay here if it hadn't been for Lila. She's the one who talked her father into hiring me."

I felt myself turn red. Mrs. McMillan deserved the job. Dad says that she's one of the best employees Fowler Enterprises has.

"You have a little girl?" Mr. Stillman asked.

Mrs. McMillan nodded. "Her name is Ellie, and she's my pride and joy," she said.

"How old is she?" Mr. Stillman asked.

"Four," Mrs. McMillan said.

"That's great," Mr. Stillman said. "Is she as pretty as you are?"

Mrs. McMillan smiled. Her eyes sparkled.

"Ellie looks just like Mrs. McMillan," I said.

Mr. Stillman grinned. "I guess that answers my question, then," he said. He reached across the table and took one of Mrs. McMillan's hands. "So," he said, "what are you doing for dinner tonight?"

Mrs. McMillan looked surprised. "Gerard Stillman, are you asking me for a date?"

Mr. Stillman scratched his head, as if he were confused. "I thought that's what I was doing," he said.

Mrs. McMillan and I laughed. Then the smile faded from Mrs. McMillan's face. "I'd love to go to dinner with you," she said, "but I'd never be able to get a baby-sitter for tonight."

Mr. Stillman nodded. "OK," he said. "Then how about tomorrow night?"

Mrs. McMillan fiddled with her straw. "I, uh, already have plans for tomorrow night," she said.

Mr. Stillman glanced at me, and then back at Mrs. McMillan. "Are you free the day after tomorrow?"

Mrs. McMillan looked really uncomfortable. "I don't think so," she muttered into her coffee.

I couldn't believe it! Mrs. McMillan was turning Mr. Stillman down right and left, but she was obviously dying to go out with him. Then it hit me: Mrs. McMillan had gone through a long period of unemployment. Her financial situation was probably still very tight. Maybe she couldn't afford a baby-sitter for Ellie!

"Mrs. McMillan, I'm free tonight. I'll baby-sit for Ellie, no charge," I said.

"Oh, Lila!" she said. "I couldn't impose on you like that."

"It's not imposing," I said. "I'd love to see Ellie. As a matter of fact, you can ask me to baby-sit anytime."

Mr. Stillman looked at Mrs. McMillan. "So?" he said.

"It looks like I have a baby-sitter for tonight after all."

Mr. Stillman grinned. "Great!" he said. "Is seven OK?"

"Perfect," Mrs. McMillan said.

Mr. Stillman glanced at his watch. "Whoa!" he said. "I'd better get back to work."

"I'll see you at seven," Mrs. McMillan said before Mr. Stillman ran off.

Mrs. McMillan and I sat at the table talking after Mr. Stillman left. She was supposed to be showing me around today, so she wasn't on as strict a schedule as usual.

"Well, that was a coincidence, wasn't it?" she said.

"An unbelievably romantic coincidence," I said. "Did you go out with Mr. Stillman for a long time?"

Mrs. McMillan nodded. "We were high school sweethearts," she said. "As a matter of fact, just before Gerard went off to college, we got engaged."

"Engaged!" I said. "But why didn't you get married?" I covered my mouth. "Oops!" I said. It really wasn't any of my business.

Mrs. McMillan laughed. "It's all right, Lila," she said. "Really. We didn't get married because Gerard wasn't ready to settle down yet. I wanted children and a home right away, and he wanted to travel, see the world. I guess he never married."

"And now Fowler Enterprises has brought you back together," I said.

Mrs. McMillan stared out the window at downtown Sweet Valley. "It's almost as if we were meant to be together. You know, fate," she said.

I couldn't help smiling to myself. Mrs. McMillan was acting all starry-eyed and dreamy, just the way Maria Slater—the Unicorn Club's very own ex–Hollywood star—had acted when she did a scene with that adorable Brad Marshall in *Secondhand Rose.* Who knew? Maybe Mrs. McMillan was right. Maybe it was fate that she and Mr. Stillman got together.

As Mrs. McMillan got ready to leave, her hand suddenly flew to her mouth. "Oh, my gosh!" she said. "I don't have a thing to wear tonight!"

I grinned. This was definitely my department. "Never fear, Mrs. McMillan," I said, pushing away from the table. "Lila's here."

Mrs. McMillan put her hands on her hips, trying to look stern. "And just what does Lila have in mind?" she asked, raising an eyebrow.

"An after-work shopping spree," I said.

Mrs. McMillan sighed. "That's very sweet of you, Lila," she said. "But if I don't have enough money to pay a baby-sitter, what makes you think I can afford to buy a new dress?"

I shrugged. "Did I say anything about a 'new' dress?" I said.

Mrs. McMillan looked confused.

"Come on," I said, "let me introduce you to the hippest vintage-clothes shop in town. Our very own vintage-clothes consultant, Mandy Miller, will—for a waived fee—dress you like a dream for practically nothing."

"Oh, I get it," Mrs. McMillan said. "You mean The Attic, right? Mrs. Willard told me the Unicorns help out there sometimes." Mrs. Willard ran the day-care center where the Unicorns volunteered.

"That's right," I said. "Mandy's spending the mother/daughter day with her mom. I'll just give her a call and see if she can meet us at The Attic."

"Oh, I don't know, Lila," Mrs. McMillan said. "You've done too much already, baby-sitting for Ellie and everything."

I waved her protests away. "It'll be fun," I said. "Mr. Stillman won't be able to resist you."

That seemed to clinch it. "OK," Mrs. McMillan said. "If you want, you can call Mandy when we get back to my office."

"Great!" I said. "You're not going to regret it!"

We left the cafeteria. I could tell from the way she was walking about three feet off the ground that this was the start of a big romance.

Three

I got home a little after six. The door to my dad's study was open, and I could hear him talking on the phone. I could tell from the tone of his voice that it was some business associate. I waved to him from the doorway. He covered the mouthpiece for a second and whispered, "Hi, honey." Then he swiveled his chair around and began talking to the person on the other end of the phone.

I sighed and went into the kitchen for something to drink. Maybe he wouldn't be so busy later. I really wanted to tell him about the take-your-daughter-to-work day.

"How did everything go?" Mrs. Pervis asked when I walked into the kitchen. She was cleaning lettuce at the sink.

"It was fun, I suppose," I said. "Too bad Mrs.

McMillan isn't a fashion photographer or a famous actress or something. All in all, I've decided computers are pretty boring." I found a can of soda in the refrigerator, and Mrs. Pervis handed me a glass.

"Oh, by the way," I said, "Mrs. McMillan is dropping Ellie off tonight. She's got a date. You'll never believe how it happened. It was so amazingly romantic. She ran into an old boyfriend at work today—really, we came around this corner and they smashed into each other. Anyway, he asked her out. So I told her I'd baby-sit."

Mrs. Pervis lifted an eyebrow. "That was awfully nice of you," she said.

I knew she was surprised, but I shrugged as if it were no big deal. It was sort of nice of me, though, wasn't it? "The guy Mrs. McMillan's going out with works for Dad, too," I told Mrs. Pervis.

"Really?" Mrs. Pervis said distractedly, as she added wine to a pan in which she was sautéing some shrimp.

Clearly, Mrs. Pervis was busy. But I didn't feel like going up to my room. I wanted to . . . I don't know. I guess I just wanted to talk to someone. You know, tell them about my day. Other kids did that. But most days when I got home the mansion was empty except for Mrs. Pervis. And she was always busy with something. If Dad was even here, he was always in his study on the phone.

Mrs. Pervis reached around me for the container of bread crumbs. "Lila, honey, why don't you go on up to your room? Dinner will be ready in fifteen minutes."

"Why so early?" I asked. We usually didn't eat until seven.

"Your father has to go to New York for a couple of days," Mrs. Pervis explained. "His plane leaves at nine."

"Oh," I said, disappointed. I hadn't expected Dad to leave on another business trip so soon. It seemed that he was traveling more than ever lately. I hardly saw him anymore. Mrs. Pervis looked at me sympathetically. I guess my disappointment showed on my face.

Well, at least I'll have Ellie for company tonight, I thought, as I headed for my room.

An hour later, I was in my room leafing through one of my favorite clothing catalogues while I waited for Ellie. Of course, I can shop wherever I want. I like the catalogues, though. First because their clothes are pretty cool, and also because you get to see a whole look, not tops over here and pants over there, like in stores.

I had just checked off the fifth outfit I wanted when I heard the echo of the doorbell chiming through the foyer. It must be Mrs. McMillan and Ellie!

I hurried down the staircase to the foyer. Mrs. Pervis was just opening the door when I reached the bottom step.

"Good evening," she said to Mrs. McMillan and Mr. Stillman.

"Good evening," Mrs. McMillan said, looking a little taken aback by the size of the foyer, not to mention the grand staircase that swept down from the second floor. Then she spotted me. "Hi, Lila!" she said.

"Hi. You look great!" I said, taking in the outfit that Mandy had picked out for Mrs. McMillan that afternoon. It was a straight, peacock-blue dress with a mandarin collar, a pair of delicate gold sandals, and a hair comb with a spray of artificial flowers. Mandy thought the dress probably came from one of Clara Kim's movies. Clara Kim is Evie's grandmother and a famous movie actress. She owns The Attic. Mrs. McMillan's outfit wasn't as funky as Mandy's usual ensembles, but she had shied away from the man's pin-striped suit jacket, oversize shirt, stretch pants, and bowler hat that Mandy had picked out for her at first.

After I said hello to Mrs. McMillan, I turned to Ellie. "How's my little munchkin?" I asked, bending down to give her a hug. She giggled and hugged me back. A feeling like warm rain bubbled inside me. I stood up, smiling. Then I noticed the worried look on Mrs. McMillan's face.

"What's the matter?" I asked.

She looked embarrassed. "I guess I'm a little nervous about leaving Ellie," she said.

For a minute I thought she was afraid I couldn't

take care of Ellie, and it made me kind of angry. It wasn't like I'd never looked after Ellie before. What about all those hours at the day-care center? Then I realized that she was probably just nervous about the evening in general.

I stroked Ellie's hair. "Don't worry, Mrs. McMillan," I said. "We'll be just fine." I smiled at Ellie. "Won't we, Ellie? We'll play and read and watch some cartoons on the huge TV. And your mom will be back in no time."

Mrs. McMillan smiled, but she still looked a little worried. "Ellie will be fine, Linda," Mr. Stillman said.

Mrs. McMillan sighed. "Of course she will," she said. Then she reached into her purse—a gold evening bag that she told Mandy she had bought for her senior prom—and handed me a slip of paper. "This is the number of the restaurant we're going to," she said, pointing to the top line. She pointed below that. "This is the name of Ellie's doctor." Her finger moved down. "And here are all Ellie's vital statistics—height, weight, birth date— in case of an emergency," she added anxiously.

I took the note and called to Mrs. Pervis, who had headed back into the kitchen. "Will you tack this on the bulletin board, please, Mrs. Pervis?" I asked.

"My pleasure, Lila," Mrs. Pervis said, taking the note.

Mrs. McMillan still seemed reluctant to leave.

"Is there anything else?" I asked.

Mrs. McMillan glanced anxiously at Mr. Stillman and then back at me. "I prefer that she doesn't have any C-O-O-K-I-E-S," she spelled out, "or C-A-N-D-Y before bedtime. And give her milk or juice instead of S-O-D-A."

I felt a flash of irritation. Did she think I was going to turn Ellie into a junk-food addict? "I'll make sure not to give her anything that isn't completely wholesome. Is that it?" I asked.

Mrs. McMillan's brow furrowed. "I think so . . ." she said.

Mr. Stillman smiled indulgently. "Does that mean we're ready to go now?" he asked.

"Yes, of course," Mrs. McMillan said. She turned to leave, and I was just about to shut the door when she turned back again. "Oh, goodness!" she said. "I almost forgot!" She dug into her purse again and pulled out another slip of paper. On it were the numbers of the police and fire departments.

I couldn't help smiling. "Mrs. Pervis has these numbers, too, Mrs. McMillan," I said.

She laughed uncertainly. "I guess I'm just a little nervous."

"Don't worry," I said, smiling at Ellie. "I know what to do in an emergency, and Ellie and I are best buddies, right, Ellie?"

Ellie giggled. "Yes," she said, hugging my leg. "I like Lila."

Mrs. McMillan's worried smile softened. "I know you do, sweetheart," she said, bending down to kiss Ellie's cheek. She smiled gratefully at me. "We'll be back in a couple of hours," she said.

"Have fun!" I said. Ellie and I waved good-bye. Then we went inside.

"This must be the famous Ellie McMillan!" my dad said fifteen minutes later. Ellie and I were reading some of my old children's books in the den when Dad joined us. "I'm really sorry I didn't get to see Mrs. McMillan," he told me. "There was an emergency in one of our European offices, and I had to take care of it."

"That's OK," I said, returning Ellie's grin. It usually made me furious when Dad ignored me on account of business, but somehow it didn't bother me so much tonight. I was having too much fun with Ellie.

Dad stooped down to give Ellie a pat on the head, then he glanced at his watch. "My plane leaves in a little over an hour," he said. "I'm going to head to the airport now."

I closed the book I was reading to Ellie. "Come on, munchkin," I said. "Let's walk my dad to the door."

Dad put his arm around me as we walked. He gave me a kiss on the forehead and smiled at Ellie when Richard, our chauffer, pulled up in the limousine. "I'll call when I get to New York," he said.

"Have a good trip," I told him.

I watched until the limousine disappeared down

the winding driveway. Then I stepped back inside. Usually, the house seemed huge and empty when Dad was gone. Oh, Mrs. Pervis and Richard were usually there, and I liked them both, but it wasn't the same as having my dad around. When Dad was home, I at least felt like I was part of a family, even if he was busy in his study most of the time.

I was glad Ellie was there. With her around, I sort of felt that same sense of family that I felt with my dad. It was kind of like having a little sister.

I smoothed her hair. "Come on, Ellie," I said, taking her hand and leading her to the kitchen. "We're going to make popcorn and watch some cartoons."

Ellie's face crinkled into a smile. "I love cartoons!" she said.

I smiled back. "I got these especially for you," I said, pulling one of the sleek white kitchen chairs out from the table for her.

Usually Mrs. Pervis made the popcorn if I wanted it, so I didn't know how to use the popper. It's the old-fashioned kind of popper that you put on the stove. Mrs. Pervis came in and poured some butter-flavored oil in the bottom, let the oil heat, then added the popcorn. "Just keep turning this crank," she told me, pointing to the handle on the side of the popper. "When the popping stops, the popcorn's ready. Just make sure you turn the burner off as soon as the popcorn's finished, so it doesn't burn."

I nodded. "I will," I said as she left the kitchen. "Thanks, Mrs. Pervis." Mrs. Pervis is really strict sometimes, and protective, but she's also pretty good at knowing when to let me do things on my own.

It didn't take long for the kernels to heat and begin to explode. Ellie's eyes grew big with excitement. "That's loud!" she cried happily. "Oh, boy!"

Once the popcorn was ready, I made sure the burner was off and poured the popcorn into a big ceramic bowl.

"Come on," I said to Ellie. "It's show time!" I put the videotape into the VCR and then sat beside Ellie on the couch.

"That's a big TV!" she said, gaping at the fifty-inch television my father had just bought. "It's like watching a movie at the theater." Ellie's eyes were glued to the screen as the cartoon came on. It was a fairy tale about a princess who ran away from home because of her evil stepmother.

"That princess looks like you," I told Ellie when the princess appeared on the screen.

"No, like you!" Ellie said, grinning. But her eyes were studying the princess. "Can I see my face?" she asked a moment later.

"Sure," I said. "I'll get a mirror." I ran to my room and came back a moment later with the gold hand mirror that went with my vanity set.

Ellie looked from the mirror to the cartoon and then back again.

"See?" I said.

Ellie frowned. "But she's got makeup on," Ellie said, pointing to her eyelids.

I smiled. "That's eyeshadow," I told her.

Ellie looked up at me with her huge brown eyes. "I like eyeshadow," she said.

"Is that a hint?" I asked, laughing. She nodded with enthusiasm. "In that case," I said, "you guard the popcorn while I get my makeup bag."

Ellie grinned and put her hands over the popcorn bowl. "Good," I said. "I'll be right back."

"Did you like that cartoon?" I asked Ellie later as the tape rewound. Ellie batted her lashes at me and looked at herself for the umpteenth time in the mirror.

"I look like Princess Rose," she said with a smile, as she ran a finger across the eyeshadow that covered her eyelids. Then the smile faded. "Why did her mommy hate her?" she asked.

"It wasn't her mommy," I said, "it was her stepmother. And she didn't like Princess Rose because she wanted Princess Rose's daddy all to herself."

"Oh," Ellie said. She thought about it for a moment. Then she glanced at her reflection. "Can I wash my face now?" she said.

"Why, don't you think you look pretty anymore?" I asked.

Ellie shook her head, a serious look on her face. "I think I want to look like me again," she said.

"I think I like you better that way, too," I said, leading Ellie to the bathroom closest to the den.

We put on a cartoon about a little yellow bird and a cat after that. Ellie fell asleep in my lap about ten minutes into it. A short while later, Mrs. McMillan and Mr. Stillman arrived to pick her up.

"How was she?" Mrs. McMillan asked as she gathered the sleeping Ellie from the couch in the den.

"She was great," I told her. "You can ask me to baby-sit anytime."

Mrs. McMillan smiled gratefully. "Thank you, Lila," she said.

I walked Mrs. McMillan to the door, then watched until Mr. Stillman's car disappeared down the driveway, just as I had watched Dad's limousine disappear. Then I went back inside and up the stairs to my room.

An hour later, I closed the history book I'd been trying to read and turned off the light. But even though I was tired from a long day, I couldn't seem to get to sleep. Instead I lay in my bed, thinking about Ellie and the special bond between mothers and their children. After all the time I'd spent with Ellie, I thought I sort of understood how they felt. I tried hard to be gentle and patient with Ellie, just as a mom would be. And she was always such a perfect angel for me—so sweet and affectionate, never any trouble.

Mrs. Riteman was full of it, I decided. Just like Ellen's usually full of it. Mothering is easy. You just have to not be a creep like Mrs. Riteman. If you treat children the way you'd like to be treated, they'll treat you well in return.

I decided that when I become a mother I will never be bossy or impatient. I'll follow Mrs. Wakefield's advice: "Mean what you say," "Keep your promises," "Be consistent and trustworthy." That's why Mrs. Wakefield is such a good mother. She treats Jessica, Elizabeth, and Steven fairly. She doesn't break promises the way my dad sometimes does.

I felt a twinge of guilt at that last thought, as though I was being disloyal to my dad. I know he can't help it when he breaks a promise, but it still hurts. Like the time he couldn't take me to the circus when I was a little kid, because some business emergency came up. Mrs. Pervis ended up taking me, but it wasn't the same.

I'll never break my promises, I vowed. My children will know what to expect. They will be polite and well behaved, because we'll understand each other. They'll never whine or talk back or make fun of me behind my back the way Ellen makes fun of Mrs. Riteman. We'll be friends. We'll play together and spend a lot of time going to the zoo and museums and the carousel in the park. Most important, I'll be there whenever they need me. I closed my eyes and began to drift off. Someday, I'm going to be a perfect mother.

After all, I thought before I finally fell asleep, how hard can it be?

Four

"I have a question about this mother/daughter day essay," Ellen said, taking a bite of her ham sandwich at lunch on Tuesday.

"Shoot," Jessica said, pitching an apple core into the trash can near the Unicorner.

"Exactly how many pages does it have to be?"

I rolled my eyes. Not this again! I thought we were through talking about the mother/daughter day. It was practically all I heard about yesterday.

"Just write it, would you, Ellen?" I said.

Ellen made a face. "I want to get an A, if you don't mind," she said.

Evie swallowed a bite of her chicken sandwich. "I don't think it matters how long it is," she said, "as long as it's well written."

"Really?" Mary said, with a toss of her long

blond hair. She grinned. "Well, then I'm all set! I'm just going to write that my mom is numero uno. The best."

Jessica frowned. "Everybody thinks their mom is the best," she said.

Mary shrugged. "Yeah, but my mom is. She never yells at me, and whenever I need to talk to her, she takes the time to really listen."

Jessica's eyes flashed. "What makes you think our mom yells at us?" she said. "And we can talk to our mom, too. Right, Lizzie?"

Elizabeth nodded. "But I don't think this essay is supposed to be a contest to find out who's got the best mother," she said.

"Spare us the lecture, Elizabeth," Ellen said.

Maria frowned. "Elizabeth's right," she said. "We all think our moms are great, so why argue about it? We're not going to change anyone's mind."

"Right," Evie agreed. "I mean, I think my grandmother is the best mother anyone could ask for. She's taken care of me ever since my mom died. I wouldn't know my mom if it weren't for my grandmother telling me stories about her. But that has nothing to do with the mother/daughter day."

"Exactly," Mandy said. "This essay is about the kind of work our mothers do, not about what kind of people they are." All the Unicorns nodded at this except Ellen, who pulled a peeled banana wrapped in plastic from her lunch bag, unwrapped it, and eased it apart. Running through the center was a perfect line of peanut butter.

"Maybe the essay isn't supposed to be about how special our mothers are," she said, "but check this out." She held the banana halves up for everyone to see. "My mom scraped out the inside bit by bit and replaced it with peanut butter. How many mothers would take the time to do that?"

Mary shrugged. "My mother may not be the greatest cook," she said, "but you can hire a cook."

"You're just jealous," Ellen said.

"Chill out, you guys!" Mandy said.

I stirred my yogurt. "Yeah," I said. "This is getting stupid. Besides, aren't you all exaggerating a bit? I mean, a lot of you have complained to me about your mothers at one time or another." I looked directly at Ellen when I said this. She was always complaining about how her mom pushed her to do this and told her to do that.

"That's just because we're so close," Ellen countered.

"You and your mom?" I said. "Give me a break."

Ellen frowned. "You just don't understand, Lila," she said.

Jessica looked crossly at Ellen. "Just because Lila's mom doesn't live with her doesn't mean Lila doesn't understand," she said.

"Then again," Maria added, "who does understand mothers?" The whole group burst out laughing.

I smiled, but I felt a little funny. What made mothers so special? I had my dad and Mrs. Pervis. What was so great about having a mom, as long as you had someone to take care of you? Look at the way I got along with Ellie! I mean, I was every bit as caring as a mother. Jessica was right. Just because my mom wasn't around didn't mean I didn't understand.

I looked around the table. The only problem was, everyone was always talking about things their mothers did for them as though it were a big deal, and I really didn't understand that. Personally, I thought it was stupid. I stood up. "I've got to go to the girls' room before class," I announced.

Jessica wiggled a couple of fingers. "I'll see you in English," she said.

" 'Bye, Lila," the other Unicorns said.

I reached for my books.

"Did I ever tell you guys about the time my mom ended up frosting a bake-sale cake for me in the car while she was driving?" Ellen asked the Unicorns as I gathered my things together.

"Only a million times," Mary said, laughing.

"I never heard it," Evie said, sitting forward with a big grin on her face, waiting to hear the story.

"Well," Ellen said. "It all started when our mothers were asked to make something for the school bake sale last year. . . ."

I hurried out of the cafeteria. What's the big deal about frosting a cake? I thought. Mrs. Pervis can do that.

But I couldn't help feeling maybe Ellen was right. Maybe there was something more to this mother/daughter thing that I didn't know about, something I was totally missing in my life. I hurried to the girls' room and studied myself in the mirror. I looked like any other seventh-grade girl, except maybe prettier and better dressed. Only, I didn't have a mother.

But that wasn't true. I *did* have a mother. She just didn't live with me. When it comes down to it, everyone has a mother. So what's the big deal? Then I remembered how Mrs. Wakefield had touched Jessica's hair at the mother/daughter day.

I pulled my comb out of my purse. Oh, so what? My dad touches my hair like that sometimes. When he's around. I pulled the comb through my hair, then stopped, my eyes watching the eyes reflected in the mirror. For a moment, something cold and empty touched my insides. But I pushed it away. I was just being sentimental, I decided. I'd had enough of this whole mother/daughter thing.

I put my comb back in my purse. Then, after one last check to make sure I looked perfect, I headed to English class.

The day-care center was total bedlam when the other Unicorns and I got there at three o'clock. Allison and Sandy Meyer had cornered Yuky Park near the playhouse and were trying to take her rag doll away. Yuky was holding her own. She had

Allison by the pigtails with one hand and was whomping Sandy with her rag doll with the other. Now I understood why Yuky's mother had bought her a soft cloth doll and not a plastic one. Evie hurried to the rescue.

On the other side of the playhouse, Arthur Foo and Oliver Washington were battling over a toy cement mixer. "It's mine!" Oliver screamed, his little brown face scrunched up with anger.

"No, mine!" Arthur countered, raising his hand to hit Oliver.

"That's enough!" Jessica said, rushing over to break up the fight.

Oliver, who adored Jessica and usually did exactly what she said, stuck his tongue out at her.

"Oliver!" Jessica said, sounding shocked.

"It's mine!" Oliver said angrily as he yanked the cement mixer out of Arthur's hands. Arthur, who'd been watching Jessica, was taken by surprise. His arms windmilled for a second, then he fell onto his behind. He just barely missed landing on a toy fire truck.

"Give me that cement mixer and apologize to Arthur!" Jessica said angrily. "Now!"

"No!" Oliver said. Then he ran toward the kitchen, with Jessica in hot pursuit. The two toddlers in the playpen added to the confusion by screaming their heads off.

Ellie, as usual, was a little angel. She was sitting in the corner. When she heard my voice, she lifted her eyes from the puzzle she was quietly putting together. Then she squealed with delight.

"Lila!" she said, running to me. "I missed you!"

I noticed Mary was watching us, and I couldn't help saying, loudly enough for her to hear, "I missed you, too, munchkin. We had an awfully good time on Friday night, didn't we? We played and made popcorn and read stories. It was fun, wasn't it?"

Ellie nodded happily. "It was a lot of fun!" she said, taking my hand and pulling me to what I'd come to think of as our corner.

I sat down in the rocking chair. A foam-rubber ball whizzed by my head as I stooped to pick up a book to read to Ellie. "Arthur, get back here!" Ellen yelled, chasing Arthur as he ran after Oliver with a foam-rubber bat.

"Look out!" Elizabeth yelled as Allison knocked over a doll carriage filled with building blocks.

Evie, holding a struggling Yuky, said, "I think there's something in the water today. These kids are acting crazy!"

Crazy was putting it mildly, I thought. I was sure glad I didn't have to deal with those other kids. Ellie was so good. Then again, maybe Ellie was good because of the way I treated her. If Ellie had been acting fresh, I would have talked to her about it instead of yelling at her the way Ellen yelled at Arthur or Jessica yelled at Oliver. I think Ellie knew that. It was a mutual-respect thing.

"Ellie isn't acting crazy," I told Evie. "It's just a

matter of knowing how to handle children."

Ellen looked exasperated. "Get real," she said. "It's just a matter of giving them time out for a month!" She glowered at Arthur.

I shrugged. "Well, it seems to me that some of us are able to handle children and some of us aren't," I said, smiling down at Ellie. Maybe it was silly, but I wanted to show the other Unicorns that I knew how to take care of kids. I didn't have to have a mom around to know how to do that.

"I think you all handle the children well," Mrs. Willard said, walking into the room. At the sight of Mrs. Willard, the children became a little better behaved. "Which is why I'm hoping you'll all come to the Center picnic on Saturday."

"A picnic?" Elizabeth said.

Mrs. Willard nodded. "We're having it in the park. Each of the parents is contributing a dish, so there'll be plenty to eat."

"It's like the potluck supper," Maria said.

"Except I can't go to the potluck supper because I'm only in the sixth grade," Evie said.

Elizabeth smiled. "But, Evie, next year you'll get to go and we'll have to stay home."

Evie raised an eyebrow. "Big deal," she said.

"Well, you're all invited to the Center picnic," Mrs. Willard said. "Mrs. Foo turned in the last of the parental permission slips this morning, and Mrs. McMillan will be coming along to help."

"That's your mom," I said to Ellie.

"Yay, Mommy!" Ellie said with a grin.

"We still have more than two weeks till Seventh Heaven Weekend," Jessica said on the way home from the Center an hour later. "I can't wait!"

"I can't wait for the potluck supper," I said. "My dad's going to be out of town on Friday and Saturday, but he promised he'd be home in time to come to the supper."

"What about the dance on Friday night?" Jessica said. "Aren't you looking forward to that?"

I shrugged.

"There'll be lots of cute boys . . ." she said temptingly. "I guess so."

"Hey," Jessica said, "I have a great idea! Why don't you stay over at my house that weekend?"

"Your house?" I said. I hadn't slept over at Jessica's house in ages.

"Sure," she said. "Why not?"

I grinned. It would be fun staying at the Wakefields'. There was always so much confusion there—Steven running off to basketball games, Jessica and Elizabeth and their friends banging around. Plus Mr. and Mrs. Wakefield. It was a big change from the echoing rooms of my house. And Mrs. Pervis had mentioned that she'd like to visit her daughter in Sunshine Falls that weekend.

"Sure," I said. "That sounds great."

"Cool," Jessica said. "I'll tell my mom you're

staying over so she can make something special for dinner Friday night."

"You don't have to do that," I said. Actually, I liked eating dinners at my friends' houses because the food tended to be so ordinary. Dad wouldn't think of letting meat loaf through our dining room door.

"Oh, my mom will love making a fancy dinner," Jessica said. "She says you're the only one who appreciates gourmet cooking. Besides, she gets a kick out of doing special things like that."

For a moment, I felt jealous. I wondered what it would be like to have someone around who liked to do special things. When we wanted a special dinner, we hired a caterer. But I put it out of my mind. No one put together a better dinner party than Mrs. Pervis. If anything, my friends should feel jealous of me.

We were at my house. "Do you want to come in for a few minutes?" I asked Jessica.

Jessica frowned. "Oh, Lila, I'd really like to, but I'm supposed to meet Aaron Dallas at Casey's in a few minutes." She smiled coyly. "We haven't spent any time with each other for a while," she said. Aaron was Jessica's sort-of boyfriend.

"OK," I said. "I'll see you tomorrow, then."

After Jessica ran off, I trudged up the driveway. I felt tired all of a sudden. I told myself it was from walking home from the day-care center instead of calling Richard for a ride, but it was a different kind of tired, a lonely tired.

That night I ate dinner by myself. Mrs. Pervis had to go out for a few hours to visit a sick friend. She'd made sole amandine, one of my favorites, but I hardly tasted it. Sitting in the big dining room, listening to the tick of the grandfather clock, I couldn't help thinking that as much as I loved sole amandine, tonight I would have preferred meat loaf.

Five

"Why don't we put the cooler over there?" I suggested to Evie on Saturday at the park. I pointed to a picnic table underneath a shady tree. It was a beautiful day for a picnic—warm and dry and not a cloud in the sky.

"Is this big enough to hold all the drinks we'll need for the day?" Evie asked skeptically.

I laughed. "This is just for the milk," I said. "Mrs. Willard's bringing a barrel full of ice for the fruit punch and sodas."

We carried the cooler over to the picnic table and set it down with a thud. "Whew!" Evie said. "That was heavy. What next?"

I looked around the park. Mary and Ellen were setting up a play area with blocks, trucks, dolls, balls, and twenty bottles of bubble solution and bubble blowers. Elizabeth and Mandy and Maria were putting down picnic blankets, and Jessica was checking out the safety straps on the toddler swings to make sure they were in good condition.

"It looks like we're all set until the food arrives," I told Evie.

We sat down on the picnic table bench to relax for a few minutes. Then we saw the Center's van winding its way toward the picnic area. Mrs. Willard was driving and Mrs. McMillan was sitting in the front passenger seat. Mrs. Willard beeped the horn several times after she brought the van to a stop.

"Come on, girls!" she said. "We've got a lot of unloading to do."

"So much for rest and relaxation," Evie said, as a minivan full of kids pulled up behind the Center's van.

Elizabeth and Mandy and Maria corralled the group of screaming preschoolers who piled out of the minivan when the driver opened the minivan door. Then they led the excited children to the playground area.

While they kept the children occupied, the rest of us helped unload the ice, charcoal, and food.

"Wow!" Evie said, lifting the aluminum foil on one of the containers of food. "Korean barbecue!"

Mrs. Willard smiled. "Mrs. Park made that," she said. "It's Yuky's favorite."

"Mine, too," Evie said.

I took a whiff of the marinated beef. "Umm," I said. "It smells delicious."

Evie nodded. "It tastes kind of like teriyaki," she said. Evie carried the Korean barbecue to the picnic table, while I lugged over a big bowl of potato salad. Mrs. McMillan carried a case of soda. Ellen struggled with a watermelon, and Mary carried a cooler full of hamburgers and hot dogs to a table near one of the park grills. Mrs. Willard carried the paper plates, paper cups, and plastic utensils.

Mrs. McMillan had just gone back for a second case of soda when a car drove up and Mr. Stillman jumped out. "I'll get that for you, Linda," he said.

"Who's that?" Ellen asked.

"That's Gerard Stillman," I told her. "Mrs. McMillan's old flame."

Ellen looked at Mr. Stillman and Mrs. McMillan. "It looks like the flame's been relit," she said.

Noticing the way Mr. Stillman was gazing at Mrs. McMillan as he carried the case of soda, I had to agree.

"Whoops!" Mr. Stillman said, staring at the shoeless child's sneaker in his hand a half hour later. "Where'd he go?"

I couldn't help giggling. Mr. Stillman was sitting at a picnic table near the playground where he'd been trying to put Arthur's sneaker on. Arthur had lost it going down the slide.

Before Mr. Stillman could get the sneaker back

on, Arthur had twisted away from him and scrambled on top of the table to get a bubble blower. Mr. Stillman grabbed Arthur's ankle before the boy had a chance to get away.

"Let's try this again," Mr. Stillman said, sitting Arthur on the table in front of him.

He got the sneaker onto Arthur's toes. Then Arthur flipped over onto his belly and began to shimmy across the table again. The sneaker dangled from his toes for a second, then fell to the ground.

"Oh, boy," Mr. Stillman said, running a hand through his hair.

Mrs. McMillan began to laugh. "I'll tell you what, Gerard," she said. "You get the sneaker and I'll get Arthur."

Gathering Arthur up as he tried to run off toward the swings without his sneaker, Mrs. McMillan planted him firmly on her lap. Mr. Stillman handed her the sneaker, and with one swift movement, she had Arthur's sneaker on. Then, holding the sneaker laces firmly, she tied them in a double knot. "That ought to hold you," she said, sending Arthur happily off to the swings.

Mr. Stillman shrugged good-naturedly. "So that's how you do it," he said.

Mrs. McMillan tousled his hair. "You'll learn," she said.

Ellie, who had been standing by the swings watching Mr. Stillman and Mrs. McMillan take care of Arthur, ran over. "My sneaker's untied!" she said to her mother.

Mrs. McMillan pulled her gaze from Mr. Stillman and glanced down at Ellie's sneaker. "No, it's not, Ellie," she said, returning her gaze to Mr. Stillman.

Ellie tugged on her mother's shirtsleeve. "It's loose!" she insisted. Mrs. McMillan sighed and looked at Mr. Stillman, who shrugged.

"I guess you should take care of your little girl," he said, rising from the picnic bench. "I'll get us some S-O-D-A-S."

"What's some S-O-D-A-S?" Ellie asked.

Her mother retied her sneaker. "It's something for Mr. Stillman and me," she said. "Now you go off and play. Gerard and I have some things we need to talk about."

Ellie turned away from her mother, a pout on her face. I hurried over to her. "Come on, munchkin," I said, taking her hand. "Let's go play on the swings."

Ellie brightened. She loved for me to push her on the swings.

We took the swing beside Oliver, who was being pushed by Jessica. As soon as I got Ellie seated, Jessica said, "Wow, Mrs. McMillan and Mr. Stillman really like each other, don't they?" She gave Oliver a good push, sending him squealing back and forth.

I glanced over at the picnic table, where Mrs.

McMillan and Mr. Stillman were sipping their sodas, their hands intertwined. "Didn't I tell you about them?" I asked, making sure Ellie was holding on tight before I set her swing in motion.

"Tell her about who?" Ellen asked. She and Sandy had just joined us at the swings.

I motioned for them to come closer. "Mrs. McMillan and Mr. Stillman used to be engaged," I whispered.

"Engaged!" Ellen practically screamed.

Jessica's mouth dropped open.

"Shhh," I said, looking over at the picnic table, where Mr. Stillman and Mrs. McMillan had let go of each other's hands and were getting ready to feed a couple of the toddlers.

"Who's engaged?" Elizabeth asked, as she and Maria approached the swings, leading Allison and Yuky by the hand.

Mary, Evie, and Mandy hurried over, carrying the three toddlers they were minding. "Wait!" Mary said. "We want to hear this, too."

I waved them in closer. "Mrs. McMillan and Mr. Stillman were engaged a while ago," I whispered. I glanced at Ellie, who was contentedly swinging back and forth. "They broke it off because Mr. Stillman didn't want children."

The other Unicorns glanced uncomfortably at Ellie.

"But I guess he likes them now," I added hurriedly.

"Even if he doesn't know how to take care of them," Elizabeth observed wryly.

I looked at the picnic table where Mr. Stillman was struggling to feed one of the toddlers a spoonful of baby food. Most of the food was on Mr. Stillman's shirt.

We all started laughing.

Then Mandy said, "Mr. Stillman might not be that great at handling kids, but he and Mrs. McMillan make a great-looking couple, don't they?"

I smiled. "Yeah," I said, "they definitely do."

The other Unicorns and I were taking a soda break when the screams went up from the playground: "It's mine!" "No, mine!" "Mine!" "No, mine!"

Ellie and Yuky were in a tug-of-war battle over Yuky's rag doll. Evie and I immediately ran to the playground.

"Stop it!" I said, pulling Ellie away from Yuky.

Ellie struggled in my arms. "I want it!" she screamed, grabbing for Yuky's doll.

I glanced at Mrs. McMillan, but she was whispering something in Mr. Stillman's ear and didn't seem to notice.

I stooped down level with Ellie. I'd never seen her so upset.

"But, Ellie," I said, "that's Yuky's doll. There are plenty of other dolls for you to play with." I pointed to the table where the toys were. Mrs. McMillan and

Mr. Stillman were sitting nearby. They were laughing now. I couldn't believe Mrs. McMillan hadn't even noticed the racket in the playground.

Ellie glowered at the two adults. "I hate those dolls!" she cried, wriggling out of my arms and running toward the swings. I took a deep breath. I suppose Ellie had a right to act up every now and then, although I was grateful that so far the "now and thens" had been few and far between.

But I knew how to solve this. Mrs. McMillan must be used to Ellie's moods. I was sure she'd have Ellie laughing in no time. I went over to the picnic table to pick out a doll for Ellie. "Ellie seems a little upset today," I mentioned to Mrs. McMillan as I searched through the dolls for one I thought Ellie would like.

Mrs. McMillan raised her eyebrows. "Really?" she said. She glanced over at Ellie, who was pouting near the swings. "I guess she is acting a little moody today," she said, "but I think she's all right. She's probably just overexcited." She turned her attention back to Mr. Stillman.

Well, I suppose if Mrs. McMillan wasn't going to worry about it, I shouldn't either. But I knew that Ellie wasn't all right. She was clearly upset, not just moody. Something was bothering her. Mrs. McMillan simply wasn't paying enough attention.

I sighed. There was nothing I could do but take care of Ellie myself.

"Ellie," I said, running over to where she was sulkily pushing an empty swing.

She crossed her arms and pouted.

"Here's a pretty doll, all for you," I said, handing her the baby doll I'd picked out.

Ellie pushed it away. "I don't want it!" she said.

"Well, then," I said. "Would you like to blow some bubbles? We have one of those big bubble blowers so you can make a gigantic bubble."

"NO!"

"Come on, Ellie!" I said, exasperated. "You can't just sulk all day!" But that only made her pout even harder.

I took a deep breath and reminded myself that she was only four years old. "How about if we play blocks?" I suggested. "We can build a whole city, right over there in the sandbox."

"I hate blocks!" Ellie said, dropping to the ground on her behind.

That's it, I thought. What a brat! Maybe I'd just let her sit there and stew in her own juice.

I turned away. But then I caught sight of Mrs. McMillan and Mr. Stillman. Mr. Stillman was explaining something to Mrs. McMillan, and she was all wrapped up in what he was saying. She had no idea what was happening in the playground.

If Mrs. McMillan was going to ignore Ellie, I thought, how could I ignore her, too?

I turned back to Ellie, who was still sitting in the dirt, looking forlorn. This was going to take a little creativity, I decided. Now, what would get me out of a bad mood if I were Ellie?

It came to me a moment later.

I walked over to Evie. "Just play along," I said out of the side of my mouth. "Mine!" I said, grabbing the soda can Evie was holding. She looked at me strangely. Then it dawned on her what I was doing.

"No, mine!" she said.

"Mine!"

"No, mine!"

"Mine!"

Evie winked at me. "It's beginning to work. She's watching us."

I turned around and glanced at her. "Good," I said. Then I fell on my behind to the ground and began to pout.

Out of the corner of my eye I saw Ellie watching me. "Mine, mine, mine!" I said, pounding the grass.

Ellie started to giggle.

I kicked my heels up and down. "Mine!" I said with an exaggerated pout.

Ellie started laughing uproariously. Then she came running over to me. She hugged me around the neck.

I hugged her back. "That's more like it, munchkin," I said. "Now, how about that bubble maker?"

Ellie glanced tentatively at the toy table. Mr. Stillman had gone off to the food table and was busy making two plates of food.

Mrs. McMillan saw Ellie looking and waved. "Hi, sweetie!" she called.

Ellie looked at her mother, then at me, then back to her mother. She hesitated for a minute. Then she grinned. "Hi, Mommy!" she said, and she ran to the table for a hug and a kiss.

"Lila," Mrs. McMillan asked me when I joined them, "would you be able to baby-sit for Ellie tomorrow night?"

Sunday night, I had everything ready for Ellie's arrival. Mrs. Pervis had brought more of my old picture books down from the attic, the popcorn maker was ready to go, and I'd rented two more cartoon videos.

The doorbell rang shortly before eight. When I opened the door, Ellie was holding on to Mrs. McMillan's leg, her face buried in Mrs. McMillan's skirt.

"Hi, Ellie," I said, expecting her to flash that great grin at me. But she acted as if she hadn't even heard me.

"Ellie?" I said.

Her mother gave me a helpless look. "She's been acting funny all day," she said, smoothing Ellie's hair. "But she doesn't seem to have a temperature."

Just then, Mr. Stillman beeped the horn. "Hurry, Linda, or we'll be late for the show!" he called out the window.

"I'll be right there," Mrs. McMillan called back.

Ellie clung harder to her mother's leg. She obviously didn't want Mrs. McMillan to go.

"Maybe I should cancel my date," Mrs. McMillan said. She looked really upset.

"Ellie's probably just tuckered out from all the excitement yesterday," I said.

Mrs. McMillan chewed her bottom lip. "Maybe . . ." she said.

"You go out and have a good time," I said, pushing her toward the door. "We'll be fine." She hesitated. "Go on," I said.

She seemed to relax. "OK," she said. "Have fun, sweetie," she said to Ellie. "I won't be long."

Ellie didn't answer. As soon as the door closed, Ellie stuck her tongue out at me and ran toward the den.

"Ellie!" I said, running after her. She'd never done anything like that before. She was acting as naughty as Sandy and Allison Meyer.

I was just about to scold her for being bratty when I caught myself. The other day at the Center, I'd told myself that I would never scold Ellie. *We had a good relationship because we had mutual respect*, I remembered thinking.

I sat down on the couch. "Come here, munchkin," I said.

"No!" Ellie shot back.

"OK," I said. "Hey, look what I've got!" I said, picking up one of the new cartoon videos from the coffee table.

Ellie looked at the videotape and then at me. She took a step forward and reached for it. *Good*, I thought, *she's interested in the tape.* I let it go.

As soon as she got hold of it, she threw it on the floor. "Ellie!" I said, trying to keep my voice even. "That wasn't a very nice thing to do."

"I hate it!" she said.

"But it's Harry and Heather," I said. Harry and Heather are a cat and mouse. They're Ellie's favorite.

"I don't care!" she said. "I hate it!"

I sighed. *OK, OK. Stay calm*, I told myself. "Hey, Ellie," I said. "Guess what I've got in the kitchen?"

She folded her arms across her chest and glared at me.

"I've got popcorn," I said when it became obvious she wasn't going to answer. "You want to help me make it?" I asked.

"No!"

I put my elbows on my knees and rested my chin in my hands. This was getting ridiculous. Mutual respect or no mutual respect, I didn't have to take this abuse. Ellie might be mad at her mother for going out, but she shouldn't take it out on me. Maybe I should just turn her over to Mrs. Pervis.

I stood up, ready to run to Mrs. Pervis's room and tell her I just couldn't handle Ellie tonight and would appreciate it if she took over. Then I remembered all the times my dad had turned me over to Mrs. Pervis because he was too busy.

I took a deep breath and lifted my head from my hands. What would Mrs. Wakefield do? I wondered. She'd talk to Ellie, that's what she'd do.

I looked over at Ellie, who was sitting on the rug, sulking. I had a pretty good idea why she was acting the way she was. Her mother had been going out a lot lately. That was obviously the reason she'd been acting so clingy tonight when Mrs. McMillan dropped her off.

I cleared my throat. "Ellie," I said, "I'm going to tell you something about me that you might not know. About me and my daddy." Ellie didn't say anything, but her eyes shifted toward me. "My daddy is a businessman," I said. "And because of his business, he has to leave me alone a lot. I hate it when he does that. It makes me feel like he doesn't love me."

The pout faded from Ellie's face, and she took a step toward me. "Your daddy doesn't love you?"

"Come here," I said, patting the couch beside me. Ellie ran over to me.

"My daddy does love me. He loves me very much. But he's a businessman. Traveling is part of his job. There's nothing in the world that he loves more than me, though, just like there's nothing in the world that your mommy loves more than you."

Ellie thought about this a minute. She frowned. "She likes Mr. Stillman better than me."

I put my arm around her and pulled her close. "No, she doesn't, Ellie. You're your mommy's little girl. No one can ever take your place. But grown-ups sometimes need to talk to other grown-ups. They need friends, just like you need friends. You wouldn't want your mommy to stop having friends, would you?"

Ellie looked up at me with her huge brown eyes, and shook her head slowly. "No . . ." she said.

"Well, then you have to let Mommy see Mr. Stillman. It would make her sad if she couldn't see him anymore."

Ellie thought about this a minute. "I could be Mommy's friend," she said.

I smiled and squeezed her. "You're Mommy's little girl," I said. "That's a very special person to be."

"It is?" she asked uncertainly.

I nodded. "It sure is," I said. "Now how about that popcorn?"

"OK," Ellie said. We started for the kitchen. But halfway there, Ellie stopped.

"What's the matter?" I asked.

Ellie frowned. "Where's your daddy now?" she asked.

"He had to go away," I said. "On a business trip."

"Like last week?" Ellie asked.

"Yes," I said.

"He loves you, but he still goes away?" she asked.

I forced a smile. "Yes," I said.

Ellie thought about that a minute. "Oh," she said at last.

"Are you ready to go make popcorn?" I asked.

Ellie nodded. "Yes," she said. But she didn't giggle the way she had the last time we made popcorn. This was more serious than I thought.

Six

It was Saturday. A week had gone by since the Center picnic, and I had hardly seen the other Unicorns outside of lunch or the classes we shared. I had to do a major book report for English. Jessica, Mary, and Ellen had a huge math test. Maria had play rehearsals. Elizabeth had to work on a late-breaking story about a new school superintendent for the *7 & 8 Gazette.* And Evie had another violin recital. On top of it all, homework seemed to have tripled for all of us. We even had to skip our weekly Unicorn meeting!

I was really glad when Saturday finally rolled around. Dad was still out of town. I always miss him when he's gone, but this week I felt really lonely, because I wasn't even able to hang out with my friends. The only bright spots in my whole week were the two evenings I baby-sat for Ellie.

I didn't baby-sit for very long, though. Mrs. McMillan was busy trying to get the rest of the Fowler Enterprises computer network up and running. She had to stay late at the office a couple of evenings. I took care of Ellie until Mrs. McMillan got out of work, but it was only for an hour each time. At least Ellie seemed to be her old self again. She was a lot of fun.

But even though it had been lonely, I'd made it through the week, and today I would finally have fun with my friends. I checked my blue leather skirt and my blue-and-white flowered cashmere sweater in a full-length mirror. I was meeting the Unicorns at Casey's in a little while.

Satisfied that my outfit looked great (Dad had bought the sweater in Paris), I added a little mascara to my lashes and some sheer-pink lipstick to my mouth, and called Richard over the intercom. "I'll be downstairs shortly," I told him. "Please have the car ready."

Casey's is this funky, old-fashioned ice cream parlor where the Sweet Valley Middle School students hang out. Besides the decor—which is really homey and warm—I liked Casey's because the ice cream is great.

The other Unicorns were already there when I arrived. They were sitting at a corner booth, sipping sodas.

"Hey, Unicorns!" I said, weaving my way through

the lacy white-metal tables and chairs positioned around the room.

"Hi, Lila!" Jessica said. She scrunched in to make room for me.

"Did you guys order yet?" I asked.

Ellen rolled her eyes. "Please, Lila, do we look like social inepts? We were waiting for you."

Jessica pushed a soda toward me. "I ordered this for you, though," she said.

"Thanks," I said.

The waitress came by a few minutes later, and we ordered our ice cream.

"Boy, this was some week, wasn't it?" Maria said when the waitress left. "This is the first free minute I've had!"

"Yeah, I've been major-league crazy," Mandy added. "Plus Archie was a regular terror this week, and Saint Cecilia had more tests than I did. Talk about tense!"

Archie is Mandy's redheaded little brother, and "Saint Cecilia" is her straight-A older sister. Their house is kind of small, so I could see how they might get in one another's hair.

"If you think little brothers are bad," Jessica said, "try having an older brother. Steven was driving us crazy this week with his junior varsity basketball talk. Every other word out of his mouth was basketball. Basketball this, basketball that."

Elizabeth nodded. "It was like living with the NBA," she said.

Evie giggled.

"At least it's Saturday," I said, taking a sip of my soda.

"Yeah," Mary agreed. "No studying until tomorrow."

"That's for sure," Evie said.

"I've got studying to do today," Ellen said with a sigh. "My mother wants me to join the French Club."

"But you don't speak French!" Jessica said.

Ellen made a face. "That's why I have to study," she said. "On top of tutoring me, Mom's got tapes of people talking French going all the time."

"What a drag," Mary said.

"My dad thinks so, too," Ellen said. "He says the tapes are driving him crazy. He's ready to move to a hotel!"

"Maybe Lila will let him borrow one of the spare rooms at her house until you learn French," Mary suggested with a grin.

"Yeah," Mandy said. She sighed longingly. "That place is as quiet as a library."

"You're so lucky, Lila," Maria said. She shook her head. "You haven't heard annoying tapes until you've lived with Nina. If I have to listen to one more song from her golden oldie collection, I'm going to scream!"

"Doo-wop, doo-wop," Elizabeth sang.

"Oh, please," Maria groaned.

Evie giggled.

I shrugged nonchalantly. "I guess I am lucky," I

said. But I wondered for a moment what it would be like to have sisters and brothers running around, playing records and talking about basketball. I quickly decided it would be awful. Who wanted to live in a zoo? And my house isn't *that* quiet—not all the time, anyway.

"Here we are!" The waitress interrupted us a few seconds later. "Now, which one of you has the strawberry sundae?" she asked, looking from Jessica to Elizabeth.

"I do," Jessica said.

The waitress nodded and placed the strawberry sundae in front of Jessica and a pineapple one in front of Elizabeth. She gave Evie a hot-fudge sundae with peppermint ice cream, and Mary and Ellen had root beer floats. There was a marshmallow sundae for Mandy, and a dusty sundae for Maria. I had ordered a double scoop of praline pecan ice cream. There was more than enough fat in that without adding whipped cream and nuts.

It was good to be with my friends, I thought, glancing around the table as the talk turned to whose ice cream looked the best. Even though I really wouldn't want to live with all the family confusion they did, I couldn't help thinking how nice it would be to have someone besides the hired help waiting for me when I got home. But my dad wouldn't be home until Tuesday. I sighed. As much as the Unicorns might envy my privacy, they didn't realize how really lonely an empty mansion could be.

*   *   *

The weekend passed in no time flat, and it was back to school again. I didn't mind. I was getting tired of being home by myself. Besides, it was Tuesday afternoon and soon I'd get to see my dad.

Richard was out front waiting for me when I left school. "Where to, miss?" he asked as I climbed into the backseat of the limo.

"Did my father get home yet?" I asked.

Richard smiled at me in the rearview mirror. "Yes, miss. His plane arrived at one o'clock."

"Home, then," I said.

As soon as Richard stopped the car, I jumped out of the backseat, not even waiting for him to open the limo door for me. I hurried into the house.

"Where's Dad?" I asked Mrs. Pervis, who was coming down the sweeping staircase.

"He's in his study," she said with a smile.

I ran to the study doorway. Dad was talking on the phone. "I'll bring the papers tonight," he was saying. "No, it shouldn't take more than a week, but we've got to act fast." He tapped a gold pen on the leather desk blotter as he spoke. "OK, John. Sure," he said. Then he hung up.

"Dad?" I said. I wanted to tell him how much I had missed him and ask him what he thought we should bring to the potluck supper on Sunday. But the phone warbled as soon as he disconnected the first call.

"I'll be with you in a minute, Lila," he said,

holding up a finger before he answered the phone. "Well, hello, George!" he said, breaking into a smile. "How're things at Sanders and Company?" He laughed. "I understand, believe me. So what can I do for you?"

I waited in the doorway for a few minutes, but Dad's minute was taking a lot longer than sixty seconds. Finally, I went to my room. At least he was home. Now I could really look forward to Seventh Heaven Weekend. It was only three days away!

"Lila, dinner's served," Mrs. Pervis said after knocking on my door a few hours later.

"I'll be right there," I said.

Hurriedly, I fixed my hair in the mirror and checked my new outfit, a pale-green denim skirt and matching embroidered denim shirt that set off my brown eyes. Then I ran down the winding staircase.

My father was sitting at the head of the table when I entered the dining room. "Hello, Lila," he said as I walked up to give him a kiss. "How's my girl?"

"Fine," I said. "Did you have a good trip?"

"It went very well," he said, signaling for the butler to start serving the veal piccata. "So what have you been doing with yourself while I was away?"

I told him about the Center picnic, my book report, and baby-sitting for Ellie. "I'm really looking forward to the Seventh Heaven Weekend," I said. "Especially the supper. What do you think we should bring?" I asked, taking a bite of the veal.

Dad cut into his veal. "Actually, Lila," he said, "that's what I wanted to talk to you about."

I could tell from the tone of his voice that it was bad news.

"I'm afraid there's some very important business I have to take care of in Boston," he said. "I won't be able to make it."

I swallowed the piece of veal. Suddenly, it tasted like sawdust. "Oh," I said.

Dad sighed. "I'm really sorry, honey," he said. "I don't have any choice."

I took a sip of my water. I wanted to scream. I mean, I know my dad is a really busy man, but didn't I deserve a break? I had to remind myself that he worked so hard in order to pay for my designer clothes and our mansion. "That's all right," I said. "I know you'd come if you could."

He smiled. "Of course I would," he said. "You're my daughter, Lila. That's a very special person to be."

I forced a smile. It was the same thing I had told Ellie. Only, I realized now that it didn't make you feel any better to know that you were special if the person who felt that way about you was never around.

"So who wants to get the snacks ready?" Jessica asked the next day. It was Wednesday afternoon, and all the Unicorns were volunteering at the day-care center.

"Why can't you do it, Jessica?" Ellen asked. "Are your fingers broken or something?"

Jessica rolled her eyes. "Don't be dense, Ellen," she said. "For your information, we're out of milk. I told Mrs. Willard I'd walk over to the mini-mart and pick some up."

"Well, I promised Sandy I'd finger-paint with her," Ellen said.

"Fine," Jessica snapped. "You're not the only one here, you know."

Elizabeth looked up from the changing table, where she was diapering one of the toddlers. "I've got two more diapers to go," she said, using her thumb and index finger to drop a dirty diaper into the diaper pail.

Mandy, Evie, Mary, and Maria were outside playing on the swings with Oliver, Yuky, Arthur, and Allison. I was sitting in the corner with Ellie, who was contentedly playing with a puzzle.

"I'll do it," I called to Jessica.

"Great!" she said.

I got up and started for the kitchen.

"Where are you going?" Ellie demanded.

"I've got to make snacks for everyone," I told her.

"No!" she said, grabbing hold of my leg.

"But, Ellie," I said. "Some of the children are hungry. We have to give them something to eat."

She pouted.

"Come with me," I said. "You can help."

That seemed to satisfy her. She took my hand and we walked to the kitchen.

"There's peanut butter over here," Jessica said, patting the top of a three-pound jar, "and jelly in the fridge. The bread's on the counter. I shouldn't be long."

"Fine," I said. "Everything will be ready when you get back."

Jessica took off for the twenty-four-hour store down the street, and Ellie and I began making the sandwiches. Ellie lined the bread up, and I smeared it with peanut butter and jelly. Then Ellie topped the sandwiches with a second piece of bread.

"Now, that's what I call teamwork," I said when the sandwiches were finished. Ellie grinned.

"May I have a sandwich?"

I looked down. It was Arthur, in from the swings.

I smiled at him. "We're waiting for Jessica to come back with the milk, Arthur," I said, bending down to wipe a smudge of dirt off his cheek.

Ellie jumped off the chair she'd stood on to help me with the sandwiches. She ran over to Arthur and shoved him. "Go away!" she said.

"Ellie!" I said. "Apologize to Arthur."

"No!" she said, glowering at him. "Go away!"

Arthur stuck out his tongue and ran off.

I felt a twinge of annoyance at Ellie's behavior. I hoped she wasn't going to start acting up again.

But I decided to ignore her outburst. Maybe she'd calm down if I didn't make a big deal out of it.

"Well, now," I said. "What do you say we cover these sandwiches with plastic wrap until Jessica gets back?"

"OK," Ellie said, as sweet as ever. I realized proudly that ignoring her had been the right move.

"Hey, Lila!" I felt a tug on my pants leg. "Lila!" I looked down. Sandy was holding a picture out to me. "Look what I did!"

"That's fabulous!" I said, holding her finger painting this way and that, like an art critic. "We'll have to hang this on the refrigerator when it's dry."

I carried Sandy's picture into the next room and hung it on the clothesline we used for drying artwork. Suddenly, there was a crash from the kitchen. "I'm going to tell!" Sandy yelled. "Ellen! Lila!" she screamed.

"What now?" Ellen said, running to the kitchen with me. When we got to the kitchen, I gasped.

"Don't you like my finger painting?" Ellie asked me.

I stared at the refrigerator, which was smeared from floor to handle with stripes of grape jelly. The rest of the grape jelly was lying in a heap of broken glass on the floor.

"That was a bad thing to do!" Ellen yelled, shaking her finger in Ellie's face.

I stepped between the two of them. "I'll take care of this, Ellen," I said. "Why don't you go get

Sandy cleaned up?" Sandy's fingers were still covered with paint.

"Sounds good to me," Ellen mumbled, glancing at the mess of jelly on the kitchen floor.

I took a deep breath. "Ellie," I said, "you know painting the refrigerator is wrong, don't you?" I asked.

She looked as though she was about to cry. "I only wanted to make a finger painting for you. I couldn't find any paper."

I stifled a smile. "Well, thank you for thinking of me," I said. "But next time, come and ask me, OK? I'll find some paper for you. And some real paints. Is it a deal?"

Ellie nodded. "OK," she said.

I gave her a big hug. So she was acting a little rambunctious lately. Who could blame her? She'd been through a lot in her life, what with her father and mother's divorce and being put in foster care for a while. And Mrs. McMillan had been going out a lot lately. It was understandable that Ellie might be acting a little clingy and insecure.

I smiled to myself. I had to admit, I was handling Ellie's outbursts with a lot of patience and maturity. I guess the nurturing part of my nature was coming out.

I smiled at Ellie. "Now, you go and put together a puzzle for me while I clean up this mess, OK?" I said. "Then we'll read a story until Jessica gets back."

"OK," Ellie said. For the rest of the afternoon, she was on her best behavior.

Seven

It was the first night of Seventh Heaven Weekend. Mrs. Pervis was in her room, packing to go to her daughter's, and I was packing for my weekend at the Wakefields'.

I was taking some designer jeans and a cable-knit cotton pullover for the outing tomorrow, a linen dress for Saturday evening, and a suede skirt and ruffled blouse for the supper on Sunday.

As I packed, I couldn't help thinking about the supper on Sunday. I was going to be the only one there without a mother or father. Jessica said that she and Elizabeth and Mrs. Wakefield would help me make something to bring to the supper, but it wasn't the same. Not by a long shot. The whole point of going to the supper was to introduce your parents to the seventh-grade class. I'd be a high school graduate before my dad met any of my classmates other than those he already knew.

I sighed and tucked one more pair of shoes into the pocket of my suitcase. Then I struggled with the zipper, trying to get it closed.

I had just managed to close the suitcase when there was a knock at the door.

"Yes?" I said.

"It's Mrs. Pervis," came the answer from the other side of the door.

"Come in," I said. Mrs. Pervis stepped into the room. She was carrying an overnight bag.

"My taxi's here," she said. "But I hate leaving you alone in the house. If you like, I can wait until the Wakefields come."

I shook my head. "I'll be fine," I said. "The Wakefields will be here any minute."

She looked a little doubtful.

"Really, Mrs. Pervis," I said. "Go ahead."

She seemed a little reluctant, but she finally nodded her head. "All right, then," she said. "Have a good time."

"You, too," I said.

I added the finishing touch to my outfit as I waited for the Wakefields: a pair of dangling crystal earrings that matched the crystal beads on my blue silk jacket. Beneath the jacket I wore a striped silk dress in hues of green and blue and black. A pair of blue patent-leather pumps completed the outfit. As I was fixing my hair, the phone rang.

I answered it. "Hello?"

"Hi, Lila? It's Jessica."

I felt a twinge of anxiety. What if the Wakefields weren't coming? "Hi, Jessica," I said, keeping my voice even. "What's up?"

"I just wanted to let you know that we're running a little late," Jessica said. "Is that OK? My mom was having trouble keeping her dress collar closed, and she sent my dad out to get some special kind of snap to make it work."

"That's fine," I told her. "How long do you think you'll be?"

"About a half hour or so," Jessica said.

"OK," I said. "I'll be ready."

I hung up the phone. I imagined the Wakefields' house—Elizabeth and Jessica running around, getting ready for the dance; Mrs. Wakefield dressing; Mr. Wakefield rushing off to find her the right kind of snap.

They would be laughing and talking as they passed each other in the hallway. Elizabeth would be telling Jessica to stop hogging the bathroom, and Steven would be giving Jessica and Elizabeth all kinds of grief.

They were a family. A real family.

For about the bazillionth time lately, the mansion seemed big and lonely. There were so many empty rooms with their high, echoing ceilings. No matter where I went, I was greeted with silence. There was no one to talk to unless I called someone on the phone or picked up the intercom to ask one of the servants for something. And that wasn't really talking, that was just giving orders.

Mrs. Pervis talked to me sometimes, but she was still the housekeeper, hired by Dad to do a job. She had a family of her own. On her days off, she went to see them.

For a moment, I felt as though everybody in the world had somebody but me. But I shook it off. Stop being a jerk, I told myself. Almost every girl in Sweet Valley would give anything to have what you have.

I decided to concentrate on getting psyched for the dance instead of feeling sorry for myself. I stepped in front of the full-length mirror and took another look at my outfit. I frowned. Was it all right? Maybe it was too sophisticated, too showy. The personal shopper at Mes Amis had assured me it was perfect. I thought it might be too much, but she'd said no.

Then again, it was the most expensive outfit in the store. Did the personal shopper really care if I bought the right dress or not? She probably got a commission for what she sold. Maybe she just sold me the most expensive outfit so she'd get more money. Maybe she didn't care whether or not it was the right outfit. I turned away from the mirror.

Suddenly, I felt like bursting into tears. Why couldn't my father have told his business associates he was busy this weekend? I hardly ever ask him to do things. Why couldn't he just this once have said no to one of them instead of to me? He always puts them before me. He was always gone. Didn't he ever wonder what I did when he was out of town? Did he really think Mrs. Pervis made up for my not having a mother and for him never being here?

I flopped onto my bed. Did he even really care about me? Oh, he provided for me. He had to. He's my father. But maybe he didn't like me. Maybe I annoyed him or bored him. Maybe he wished I'd never been born. Maybe that was why he was always gone.

I stared at the high ceiling of my bedroom, imagining the Wakefields bustling around their house, helping each other get ready for the dance. Right now, I'd trade my huge allowance and all my clothes—even this mansion—for one of my friends' parents. Even Mrs. Riteman! She might be a creep, but at least she was there for Ellen. At least she cared. At least she'd be at the potluck supper.

I forced back the hot tears that had begun to sting my eyes. I didn't want the Wakefields to see me all red-eyed and mascara-streaked. I didn't want them to ask me what was wrong. I went to the bathroom to get a drink of water and calm myself down.

Just then, the doorbell rang. It must be Mr. Wakefield! I glanced at my gold watch. He was early. Jessica must have told him to pick me up on his way back from the store.

I checked myself in the mirror one last time. Then, taking a deep breath, I grabbed my suitcase and ran down the stairs to answer the door. I just wanted to get out of there, to run away from the huge empty mansion with its cold rooms and echoing halls.

I paused to fix a smile on my face before I opened the door. I didn't want Mr. Wakefield to think that anything was wrong. But when I opened the door, the smile turned into openmouthed shock. It wasn't Mr. Wakefield standing there. It was Ellie! And she was all by herself!

Eight

"What are you doing here?" I asked Ellie, peering into the darkness to see if I could spot Mrs. McMillan's car. "Where's your mother?"

Ellie stared up at me, her big eyes glistening with tears. "I ran away," she said.

I gasped. I pictured Ellie crossing busy streets and intersections, trucks and cars whizzing by. I pulled her inside.

"You what!" I exclaimed. "You could have been . . . hurt!"

I hugged her tight, trying not to think about what could have happened to her. All those busy streets! But then I remembered that Mrs. McMillan's apartment complex wasn't really that far away. I mentally walked from their house to mine. Ellie only had to cross one major street, and it was a pretty quiet one. She could have followed the sidewalks to my house. I let out my breath. Still, I realized that something must be very wrong for Ellie to do something like that.

"Come inside," I said, taking her hand and leading her to the den. I sat her on the big flowered couch. "Now, tell me what's wrong," I said.

Ellie took a deep breath. "Mommy went on a business trip," she said.

"Oh," I said. I certainly knew that feeling. "Is that why you ran away?"

Ellie shook her head. "No. Mr. Stillman was at our house before Mommy left," she said, twisting the hem of her T-shirt. "I went to the kitchen to get a glass of milk. Mommy and Mr. Stillman didn't see me. They were talking about going away." She looked up at me, terrified.

"Maybe they were talking about your mommy's business trip," I suggested.

Ellie shook her head vehemently. "No," she said. "They were talking about going away together. Mr. Stillman was talking about going lots of places. He said just him and Mommy." Fat tears dropped onto her lap. "Mommy said she had to start looking for someone to leave me with."

"Did you ask your mommy where she and Mr. Stillman were going?" I asked Ellie.

She shook her head. "Then a baby-sitter came and put me to bed. I sneaked out and came here. She . . . the baby-sitter was getting a snack in the kitchen."

I didn't have to wonder how Mrs. McMillan could afford a baby-sitter to go on a business trip but not to go on a date. My dad was always telling me how supportive of families Fowler Enterprises was. When employees travel on business, the company pays for child care if necessary.

"Ellie, I'm sure your mom didn't mean she was going to give you away," I said.

"Yes, she did. She's going to leave me alone forever!" Ellie buried her face in my arm. "She doesn't love me anymore," she said. "She loves Mr. Stillman. I don't want to live with Mommy. I want to live here, with you!"

As much as I hated to see Ellie upset like this, I couldn't help feeling a little glad that it was me she'd turned to. But it was impossible for her to stay here. She belonged with her mother.

I hugged her. "It's OK," I said. "We'll straighten this out. I'm sure your mommy's not going to leave you."

But even as I told her that, I began to have my doubts. I couldn't help remembering my talk with Mrs. McMillan the day we ran into Mr. Stillman at Fowler Enterprises. Mrs. McMillan said that the reason she and Mr. Stillman hadn't gotten married was that he didn't want children and he wanted to travel. And then there was the way she'd treated Ellie at the picnic. Mrs. McMillan had practically ignored Ellie the whole day. It was as if she and Mr. Stillman didn't want Ellie around. Could that possibly be true?

Maybe Mrs. McMillan was planning to run off with Mr. Stillman and leave Ellie behind. Maybe she didn't want to miss a second chance to be with Mr. Stillman, and since Mr. Stillman didn't want children, she was going to give Ellie up. She had put Ellie into foster care once before. What was stopping her from doing it again?

But that was crazy. Mrs. McMillan loved Ellie. You just had to look at the two of them together to see that. Parents who love their children don't go off and leave them.

Then again, my father was always going off and leaving me, and he was supposed to love me.

I was so confused. I didn't know what to think.

"Lila?" Ellie had stopped crying. "I want to sleep in your room with you," she said.

"My room?" I said. "But, Ellie, you can't stay."

"Yes!" Ellie insisted. "I don't want to go home! I want to live with you forever!"

I ran a hand through my hair, wondering what to do. Ellie was obviously very upset. There must be a reason for it.

"OK," I said. "You can stay in my room, but only until I find out what's going on." But how, I wondered, was I going to do that? I supposed I should call the baby-sitter. Yes, that was the thing to do. Maybe she knew something Ellie didn't.

"And you promise not to tell anyone where I am?" Ellie asked.

I picked up the phone beside the couch. "Sure,

Ellie," I said, not really paying attention to what she said as I started to dial Mrs. McMillan's number.

"Promise," Ellie repeated.

"Yes, I promise." Then it registered. "Well . . . I mean . . . I at least have to tell the baby-sitter you're here," I said.

Ellie's face scrunched up. "But you promised!"

"I know, Ellie," I said. "But she'll be worried about you."

"I don't care!" Ellie said. "You promised, you promised!"

I remembered what Mrs. Wakefield had said about keeping your promises to children and being trustworthy. I hung up the receiver. If Mrs. McMillan really was planning to leave Ellie in foster care, Ellie would feel betrayed and unloved. She needed someone she could trust, or she might never trust anyone again! The baby-sitter probably had no idea Ellie was missing, anyway. She probably thought Ellie was in bed, asleep. I could deal with her later. "OK, Ellie, I won't tell."

I started to dial the Wakefields' number.

"Who are you calling?" Ellie demanded. "You promised."

I sighed. "I know I promised, Ellie," I said. "I was supposed to go to a dance tonight. I have to call Jessica and tell her I can't go now."

"Don't tell her I'm here!" Ellie warned.

"I won't," I said.

Mrs. Wakefield answered the phone. "Mrs.

Wakefield," I said. "It's Lila. I'm really sorry, but I've just come down with a terrible headache. I'm not going to be able to make it to the dance."

"Oh, Lila!" Mrs. Wakefield said. "I'm so sorry to hear that!"

In the background I could hear Jessica asking what was wrong. Then she got on the phone. "Lila, you have to come!" she said. "This is going to be the coolest dance of the whole year! You can't miss it!"

"I really want to go," I said, "but my head is killing me."

"Can't you take some aspirin?" Jessica asked.

I took a deep breath. "I already did," I said. "It didn't help. Mrs. Pervis is staying on to take care of me tonight. But I can still come over tomorrow night," I added.

Jessica sighed. "OK," she said. "If you can't come, you can't come. But I hate for you to miss it."

"Me, too," I said. For a second, I thought about leaving Ellie alone for a few hours. Then I could at least go to the dance for a while.

But even as I thought it, I knew I couldn't do that. Ellie was only four years old. What if there was a fire? Or she hurt herself?

"Have fun, Jessica," I said. "I'll see you tomorrow."

"See you," Jessica said. She sounded as disappointed as I felt.

"OK, munchkin, so what do you want to do now?" I asked an hour later. After I had talked to

Jessica, I changed out of my party outfit, and Ellie and I had our own party. We'd been playing CDs and dancing for the last half hour, and Ellie was back to her old, sweet self. I knew I had to somehow let the baby-sitter know that Ellie was here without breaking my promise, but actually it was kind of fun, the two of us alone in the house. Even if I did have to miss the dance.

"Let's make popcorn!" Ellie said.

I hesitated. I'd never made popcorn by myself before. But I shrugged the hesitation off. What was the big deal? You threw some oil into the popper, heated it, threw in the kernels and—poof! Popcorn!

"Come on!" I said, and we hurried off to the kitchen. I found the popper in the pantry, and the oil and popcorn in one of the cupboards. "OK, now we cover the bottom of the pan with oil," I said, remembering what Mrs. Pervis had told me. "And then we wait for the oil to get hot."

Ellie grinned up at me, and I thought how great it would be to be a mom.

When the oil started smoking, I added a half a cup of popcorn to the popper, as Mrs. Pervis had instructed, then looked inside. The kernels just barely covered the bottom of the pan. I frowned. That couldn't be right, could it? That would hardly give us any popcorn at all. "Maybe she said one and a half cups," I mumbled.

I poured another cup of popcorn into the popper and looked inside. That was more like it! I smiled at Ellie. "Now we're cooking." I giggled, dropping the flip-open cover down.

I immediately began turning the crank, to keep the kernels from burning. In a couple of minutes, the popping started. "Here goes!" I said to Ellie. She covered her mouth and laughed with delight.

Pop! Pop pop pop! Pop-pop-pop-pop-pop-pop-pop! The cover began to push up. "Almost done," I said to Ellie. I couldn't turn the crank anymore—the pan was too full.

Poppity-pop-pop-poppity-pop-pop-pop-pop-poppity! The cover began to push open. I backed up. "It must be finished now," I said to Ellie, who was openmouthed, watching the rising cover.

POP-POPPITY-POP-POP-POP-POP-POP!

"Whoa!" I exclaimed. The popcorn was beginning to pour out of the pan, with no signs of stopping.

"Wow!" Ellie said.

I rushed to the stove and shut the fire off just as popcorn began exploding from the popper. "Run!" I said, grabbing Ellie's hand and pulling her from the kitchen.

When we got to the den we stared at each other for a few seconds, then burst out laughing. "I guess it was just a half cup of kernels I was supposed to use," I said when I finally caught my breath.

"Popcorn was everywhere!" Ellie exclaimed.

I nodded. "Yeah," I said. "I guess I'd better clean it up. It should be safe now."

Ellie and I tiptoed to the kitchen, as if the popcorn might hear us and decide to attack. We stopped at the door. There was an occasional pop from the popper, but all in all, it seemed safe to go in.

I gasped when I saw the kitchen. The stove and floor were covered with popcorn. Kernels had managed to reach the counter and the sink and even the table in the middle of the room.

Ellie picked up an armful of popcorn from the floor and tossed it in the air. It stuck in her hair and the cuffs of her pants. I shook my head. "Don't do that, munchkin," I said. "How about helping me clean this up, then we'll make some more, OK?"

"OK," Ellie said.

I pulled the electric broom from the closet, and soon the kitchen looked like a kitchen again. After washing out the popper (it took me a while to find the dish detergent—Mrs. Pervis kept it underneath the sink), I poured oil into the popper's bottom and set it on the stove. This time when the oil began to smoke, I added a half cup of popcorn. Period. Soon Ellie and I were back in the den, listening to CDs and eating popcorn.

"Where are all your toys?" Ellie asked me as we munched on our snack.

"Most are in storage," I said. "But some are in my room."

"May I see?" Ellie asked.

"Sure," I said, wiping my fingers on one of the monogrammed napkins I'd found in the linen closet. "Come on."

Ellie's mouth formed a little O when I opened

my bedroom door and she saw the shelves and shelves of dolls. "Wow!" she exclaimed. "It's better than a toy store!"

I grinned. I only kept my favorite dolls in my room. There were hundreds more dolls in storage, along with my bikes, tricycles, games, and stuffed toys.

Ellie ran over to the shelves and just stared, as if she were looking through a magical storefront window. I decided then and there that all my old toys were going to the Center. "Go ahead," I said. "You can play with them."

"Really?" she said.

"Sure."

She glanced from doll to doll, then pointed to a baby doll on the top shelf. "May I play with that one?" she asked.

I followed her pointing finger with my eyes. It was Sarah, my favorite doll of the whole bunch. She had really curly blond hair and big blue eyes, and she was soft, like a real baby. No one had ever been allowed to play with Sarah but me.

"That one's kind of hard to reach," I said. "Wouldn't you rather play with this doll?"

I held out a beautiful porcelain doll with black curls and big brown eyes. "She looks like you," I said.

Ellie pouted and shook her head. "That one," she said, pointing to Sarah.

"How about her?" I asked, choosing a fashion doll with long blond hair, wearing a sequined evening gown.

Ellie shook her head and crossed her arms. "That one," she said, pointing again.

I sighed. Ellie could be very stubborn. "OK," I said. "But be very careful, all right?"

Ellie nodded happily. "All right," she said.

I had to climb onto the window seat to reach Sarah. Just as I grabbed her, I was startled by something being thrown against the window. I looked out. Jessica was standing beside her bike on the lawn.

I handed Ellie the doll, with a reminder to be careful, and flung open the window. "Hi!" I called.

"I rang the bell," Jessica said. "But I guess you couldn't hear it over the music."

"Hold on!" I said, running to the entertainment system to turn the volume down. I ran back to the window. "What are you doing here?" I asked, leaning out the window.

"I left the dance, because I felt bad about you getting sick and missing it," she said. "Everybody did."

"Gee," I said. "You shouldn't have done that."

Jessica shrugged. "That's OK," she said. "But it's really too bad you couldn't go. The band was awesome. Almost as good as Johnny Buck's band. And the gym was decorated with all these pastel-colored lanterns and crepe-paper streamers. It looked really pretty." I felt a slight pang about missing it all. But I was really touched that Jessica had left a good time like that just to keep me company.

"So, anyway," Jessica said. "How about letting

me in?" Panic shot up my spine. How could I let her in with Ellie here?

"Who's that?" Ellie demanded.

I turned away from the window. "It's Jessica," I whispered.

"Don't tell her I'm here!" Ellie said.

"I won't," I whispered.

"Who are you talking to?" Jessica asked me.

"No one," I said, waving Ellie back.

Ellie ran to my bed and began to jump on it. I gave her a stern look, but she kept jumping.

"Look, Jessica," I said. "My headache's still pretty bad. Maybe you'd better just go back to the dance."

"What?" Jessica said. "But I came to keep you company!" Before I could convince her that I needed to be alone, Ellie jumped too high on the bed, bounced twice, and then rolled onto the floor.

"Owwww!" she screamed as her head hit the carpet. Then she began to cry.

"Oh, no!" I said, covering my mouth with my hand.

Jessica frowned. "Who's up there?" she demanded. Then she squinted, looking suspicious. "Is that Ellie I hear crying?"

"No," I said. "I've got to go!" I climbed off the window seat.

"Hey, wait a minute!" I heard Jessica say as I ran to comfort Ellie. "Lila Fowler, I demand to know what's going on up there!"

Nine

"What!" Jessica gasped after I told her why Ellie was there. "You can't keep some kid hidden here!"

We were sitting in the den. I looked at Ellie, who was contentedly playing with Sarah on the rug.

"I know," I said. "But I promised her I wouldn't tell anyone she was here. I can't go back on my word."

"Why not?" Jessica demanded.

I crossed my arms. "Because," I said, "there's obviously something going on that's upsetting Ellie. She said she overheard her mother and Mr. Stillman talking about going away together."

"So?" Jessica said.

"They said they were going without Ellie," I told her. "Ellie thinks they plan to give her away—to a foster family or something."

Jessica frowned. "Maybe Ellie misunderstood," she said.

I sighed. "Maybe," I said. "But until I know for sure, I have to protect Ellie. If there is something going on, Ellie needs a friend. I promised her I wouldn't tell anyone she's here. I can't break that promise."

Jessica frowned. "I think this is between Mrs. McMillan and Ellie," she said.

I shrugged. "Even if it is, I can't break my promise to Ellie."

Jessica's eyebrows rose. "Since when are you so true to your word, Lila Fowler? You've broken more promises than most people make in a lifetime." I glared at her. "All right, all right. Maybe *I* can tell," she said. "I didn't promise."

I shook my head. "No," I said. "Ellie will still think I betrayed her. If you tell anyone she's here, she'll blame me." I sighed. "It's a matter of trust. I know I shouldn't be hiding Ellie here, but I can't tell on her. I've got to find a way of making her want to go home."

Jessica frowned, her eyes fixed on Ellie. "She seems pretty content," she said. "I don't think it's going to be too easy to make her want to go home."

"I know," I said. "But maybe I can talk her into it."

"Ellie," I said, getting down on the rug with her. "It's getting really late. Wouldn't you like to go home now, to your nice cozy bed?"

Ellie shook her head. "I want to stay with you," she said.

"But, Ellie," I insisted. "Your mommy will miss you. What if she calls and you're not there? She'll be very disappointed. And worried."

Ellie kicked her heels on the floor. "No! Mommy loves Mr. Stillman. I want to stay here with you. You promised!"

"Let me at least call the baby-sitter," Jessica whispered in my ear. "You can't have Ellie stay here."

I shook my head. "I can't break my promise."

Jessica rolled her eyes. "Li-la," she said. "That's ridiculous."

I frowned. "Not according to your mother it isn't," I said. "Your mother said that a good mother keeps her promises. She said you have to be trustworthy. I think the same thing goes for anyone who takes care of children. If I tell anyone Ellie's here, she'll never trust me again." I sighed. "I'll just have to wait till she decides to go home on her own."

"That could be a very long time," Jessica said. "I'll wait."

Jessica stood up. "Well, I'm not going to wait. If you're not going to send Ellie home, I'm going back to the dance." Ellie stuck her tongue out at Jessica.

"That's it," Jessica said. She started for the door. "I get enough of that at the Center."

Jessica started for the door, then stopped and turned around. "We can still drop Ellie off on our way to the dance . . ." she said temptingly.

I shook my head. "Forget it," I said. "Just go."

"Fine," Jessica said.

"Um, Jessica?" I said.

"Yes?" She turned to look at me.

"You have to promise you won't tell anyone Ellie's here, all right?"

Jessica rolled her eyes. "I think you're crazy," she said.

"Please?" I said.

Jessica sighed. "All right," she said. "I promise."

"Thanks," I said.

I listened to the door close behind her. I couldn't believe she was abandoning me, but I supposed I should be grateful that she at least promised to keep quiet about Ellie.

As soon as Jessica left, Ellie banged Sarah on the floor. "I don't want to go home, ever!" she whined.

I rushed to Sarah's rescue. "Don't do that!" I snapped. "You can't play with her if you're going to be rough. She might break."

Ellie pouted. "I don't like her anyway," she said. "I want something to eat!"

"Like what?" I asked wearily.

"Ice cream. I want ice cream."

"It's too late for ice cream," I said, glancing at my watch. It was nine-fifteen. Ellie should have been in bed ages ago. "You should be asleep."

"I don't want to sleep!" Ellie whined. "I'm not tired!"

I rolled my eyes. Maybe Ellie wasn't tired, but I sure was.

I plopped down on the floor beside her. "OK," I said. "In that case, let's read a story." I crossed my fingers, hoping a story would put her to sleep.

Almost an hour later, I was still reading. I couldn't believe things had gone this far. It was after ten and Ellie was still up. And cranky.

"I'm hungry!" she whined after about my fiftieth reading of *The Cat in the Hat*.

I didn't have the energy to argue. "How about a peanut-butter sandwich and some milk?" I suggested.

"OK," Ellie said.

Well, at least she wasn't complaining about that.

"I'll go make you one," I said, hoping that she'd fall asleep while I was in the kitchen. But it was as though she had radar for that sort of thing.

"I want to go with you!" she screamed.

"All right, all right," I said, noticing that the fake headache I'd used as an excuse earlier was becoming a reality. "Just stop screaming!"

"I'm not screaming," she whined.

I rolled my eyes. "OK, Ellie, have it your way," I said.

"But I'm not screaming!"

"OK, OK, you're not screaming," I said, just barely managing to keep from screaming myself.

We trudged to the kitchen. I was so tired, I could hardly keep my eyes open. Ellie, on the other hand, seemed ready to go for the rest of the night.

"OK," I said. "First we need some peanut butter."

I opened the refrigerator. Nothing. I searched the cupboards, and finally found a jar of chunky peanut butter.

"All right," I said, taking a loaf of bread from the bread box and opening the peanut butter. "One peanut-butter sandwich, coming up."

I started to spread the peanut butter on the bread. "What's that?" Ellie asked, crinkling her nose and pointing to the chunks of peanut.

"Those are peanuts," I said.

Ellie grimaced. "I don't like them," she said.

I took a deep breath to calm myself. "But, Ellie," I said, "peanut butter is made from peanuts."

"I don't like lumps!" she said, banging the table with her fist.

"Fine," I said, screwing the cover on the jar. I went to the cupboard and searched for a jar of creamy peanut butter. I pushed aside jars of truffles, imported olives, and tins of caviar. I found several jars of English marmalade and some maraschino cherries. I even found a jar of honey-roasted macadamia nuts. But I couldn't seem to find any creamy peanut butter.

Just when I thought I would have to pick the peanuts out of the chunky-style peanut butter with tweezers, I looked behind a stack of canned lobster meat and found a jar of plain old unchunked peanut butter.

"OK," I said. I spread some of the smooth peanut butter on a piece of bread. "No lumps, see?"

Ellie nodded. I covered the peanut-butter-smeared bread with another slice of bread. "There you go," I said, pushing the plate toward Ellie.

Ellie looked at the sandwich sideways, then made a face. "Too skinny," she said.

I wanted to scream. "Give it to me," I said, grabbing the sandwich.

Ellie's face fell. She looked as if she was about to cry.

"All right, all right," I said, trying to keep calm. "It's no big deal, see?" I took the top off the sandwich, spread some more peanut butter on it, and closed it again. "How's that?" I asked.

Wrong question. Ellie shook her head. "Now it's too fat," she said.

I took a deep breath and tried to keep from wringing her neck. Taking the sandwich back again, I scraped off the peanut butter bit by bit until Ellie was satisfied. Then I poured her a glass of milk.

"I want chocolate milk," she said.

I crossed my arms. "Ellie, this is getting out of hand," I said.

"Chocolate!" she screamed.

But I wasn't giving in again. Not without getting something in return. "I'll tell you what," I said. "If I give you chocolate milk, you have to promise to go to bed right after you eat."

Ellie pouted. "I'm not tired."

"Then no chocolate milk," I said.

"I want chocolate milk!" Ellie screamed.

I shook my head. "No bed, no chocolate milk," I said firmly.

Ellie stared angrily at me for a moment, but I guess she could tell I wasn't going to give in. "OK, I'll go to bed," she said meekly.

"Fine, then you can have some chocolate milk," I said, taking the syrup out of the refrigerator.

By the time Ellie finished her sandwich, she was ready for bed. The food must have lulled her, because she could hardly keep her eyes open.

I led her up to my room, and after taking off her shoes and socks, tucked her in. "Good night, Ellie," I said, kissing her on the forehead.

"Good night, Lila," she murmured.

I started to leave.

"Lila?" she called, just before I closed the door.

"Yes?"

"Remember you promised not to tell anybody I was here until I say so, OK? You promised."

I sighed. "Yes, Ellie, I remember I promised," I said, wishing the word had never been invented.

I was brushing my teeth fifteen minutes later when the doorbell rang. I glanced into my bedroom, hoping the sound hadn't disturbed Ellie. She murmured a little, but she stayed fast asleep.

I ran quickly down the stairs, and after checking to see who it was, opened the door. Jessica and Ellen stepped inside. "Is Ellie gone?" Jessica asked.

I shook my head. "I'm afraid not," I said. I glanced at Ellen, then at Jessica. "Did you tell everyone?" I asked Jessica angrily.

Jessica exhaled impatiently. "No, I didn't tell everyone," she said. "My parents didn't want me out this late by myself, so Ellen got permission to come with me. She promised not to say anything," Jessica added.

I let out my breath. "I didn't mean to snap at you, Jessica," I said. "It's just that this thing is totally out of control."

"Well, I say you call the baby-sitter right now," Ellen said, "before it goes any further."

"I can't," I protested. "I promised that I wouldn't tell anyone Ellie was here until she gave me permission to. I can't break that trust."

"But you can't keep Ellie here, either," Jessica said. "She should be home, in bed!"

"You think I don't know that?" I said, flipping my hair over my shoulders. "I'm sure after a good night's sleep she'll wake up missing her mother and want to go home. Just wait and see."

Jessica and Ellen exchanged glances.

"I really think you should call someone," Ellen said.

I rolled my eyes. "Stop saying that," I snapped. "I already told you, I'm not breaking my promise to Ellie. And neither are you."

"You don't have to get huffy," Ellen said, crossing her arms and turning her head away.

I sighed. "I'm just tired," I said. "It's been a long night."

Jessica looked around the huge hallway. "It's awfully quiet here with your dad and Mrs. Pervis gone and Ellie asleep," she said. "Kind of spooky." She tucked her hair behind her ears. "Do you want us to stay over?" She glanced at Ellen. "I mean, if that's all right with you, Ellen?"

"It's fine with me," Ellen said.

"That would be great," I said. Just having some of my friends around seemed to take some of the burden of hiding Ellie off me. At least I'd have some company.

"OK," Jessica said. "I'll call my parents and tell them Mrs. Pervis invited us to stay over."

"Me, too," Ellen said.

"Thanks, guys," I said. "I really appreciate this."

"I want cartoons!" Ellie's whiny voice woke me early Saturday morning. I glanced at the clock. It wasn't even seven-thirty yet!

"Go back to sleep," I mumbled, covering my head with a pillow.

"I want cartoons!" Ellie insisted.

"It's too early for cartoons," I said.

"Mommy lets me watch cartoons," Ellie said, shaking my shoulder.

Well, I'm not Mommy, I almost snapped. Then I realized maybe I could use that to convince Ellie to go home. It was obvious that staying here wasn't doing her any good. She and Mrs. McMillan needed to talk. I sat up. "Mommy's really nice to let you watch cartoons," I said. "I bet she misses you, too. Maybe I should call—"

"NO!" Ellie screamed before I could finish the sentence. "You promised!"

"But, Ellie," I said, "you can't stay here forever."

"You promised!" Ellie screamed. "You promised!" She began pounding the pillow with her fists and kicking the covers everywhere. Tears streamed down her face.

"All right, all right!" I said. "Calm down or you'll wake Jessica and Ellen. I'm not going to call anyone."

Ellie continued to pound the pillow and cry.

I was trying to calm her down when suddenly I heard a car in the driveway. I ran to the window. It was my father! He was back early!

I ran back to the bed. "Ellie," I said. "Shhh, it's OK. We'll watch cartoons, all right? And I won't call anyone. I promise I won't call anyone."

"You're going to tell!" Ellie wailed.

"Shhh," I said, stroking her hair. "I'm not going to tell anyone. Just please stop crying."

That brought an even louder wail from her.

I heard the car door slam and my father talking to Richard. *OK, stay calm,* I told myself, picking up Ellie's clothes and shoving them into the closet. At least hide the evidence!

But the evidence in my room was nothing compared with the evidence downstairs: peanut-butter jars . . . kids' books . . . Sarah! What was I going to do? My father would be inside any moment.

I ran from the room and knocked on the guest-room door.

"Jessica! Ellen!" I said through the door. "Help!"

Then I ran downstairs.

Ten

Ellen, Jessica, and I had barely put away the peanut butter and hidden the toys when my father walked into the house.

"Hi," the three of us said, greeting him in the front hall.

"Lila!" he said, surprised. "Hello, Jessica. Ellen." He glanced at his watch. "What are you girls doing up this early?"

"We . . . uh, we . . ." I stammered.

"We were so excited about the Seventh Heaven field day, we couldn't sleep," Jessica blurted.

"I see," my dad said. He looked a little confused for a minute, then he shrugged. "Well, have a nice time," he said. Then he disappeared into his study.

My head was spinning. What was I going to do? I'd promised Ellie I wouldn't tell anyone she was here, but I hadn't counted on my dad's coming home. Now I was going to have to hide her from him. And then there was the baby-sitter. She was probably worried sick. But Ellie didn't show any sign of wanting to go home.

"I can't believe you didn't tell him what's going on," Jessica said, shaking her head.

Ellen nodded in agreement. "Are you going to hide Ellie all day? You'll miss the field day, just like you missed the dance." She crossed her arms. "I wouldn't do that for anyone."

"Well, I would," I said. "And I'm going to hide Ellie until I can figure out a way to make her want to go home."

"Get real, Lila!" Jessica said. "How do you think you're going to keep your dad from finding Ellie today? And what about Mrs. McMillan? The baby-sitter has probably called her already. I'll bet they've even called the police."

The police? I felt the blood rush from my face. I hadn't thought about the police. Ellie had been with me for nearly twelve hours. I could probably be arrested for kidnapping!

"It doesn't matter," I said determinedly. "Ellie will lose her trust in me if I tell."

Jessica sighed. "Well, I'm going to the field day, whether you tell or not," she said.

"Me, too," Ellen agreed.

That was smart, I thought. If I got arrested, Jessica and Ellen wouldn't be dragged down with me. "I'll be OK," I said, even though I felt as if I'd never be OK again.

Jessica sighed. "Look, Lila, I know you don't want to break your promise to Ellie. We'll try to think up a solution, all right?"

"Thanks, guys," I said, feeling a little better. Then Jessica and Ellen left.

I watched them through the window, feeling like the only kid on the block not invited to a birthday party. It was bad enough I'd missed the dance. I didn't want to miss the field day, too. Especially not when I knew what was waiting for me upstairs—a cranky, tantrum-throwing Ellie, who wouldn't be quieted down. And how was I supposed to keep her hidden from my father, anyway?

I started wearily up the stairs. *Slam!* I whipped around at the sound of the front door closing.

And I thought things were as bad as they could get! Not quite. It was Mrs. Pervis.

"Mrs. Pervis," I said, running downstairs again. "What are you doing home?"

Mrs. Pervis sighed. "Oh, I'd forgotten how much my son-in-law gets on my nerves. I left early." She gave Lila a funny look. "Speaking of which, what are you doing home? Didn't you stay at the Wakefields' last night?"

I gulped. "Yes, but, uh . . . I didn't sleep very well," I said, "so I came home early."

"You couldn't sleep?" She looked concerned. If

there was one thing I didn't have trouble doing, it was sleeping.

"Uh . . . I guess it was because I was in a strange bed," I told her. "The, um, pillows were hard, and the mattress was kind of lumpy."

"Oh," she said. "I see. Well, you'll have plenty of time to get ready for the big day, then, won't you?"

I wished I could disappear into the floor. "Actually," I said, "I'm not going to the field day."

"What?" Mrs. Pervis said, setting down her suitcase. "But you've been looking forward to this weekend for months."

"I know," I said, raising my hand to my temple. "But I've got a really bad headache."

"A headache?" Mrs. Pervis smoothed my hair. "It's probably from not getting enough sleep," she said. "Come on, we're putting you to bed."

She started to lead me to my room.

"No!" I said, remembering that Ellie was up there.

Mrs. Pervis stepped back, surprised. "For heaven's sake, why not?" she asked.

I swallowed the lump in my throat. "My, um, head's starting to feel better already," I said. "Maybe I'll go to the field day after all."

Mrs. Pervis's eyebrows drew together suspiciously. "Lila, is there something going on I should know about?" she asked.

I almost choked. "No!" I said, forcing a smile. "Of course not. Everything's just great." Except that any minute now, Ellie will probably come downstairs and I'll be up a creek without a paddle. "As a matter of fact, Dad came back early," I said, trying to divert Mrs. Pervis's attention.

"He did?" she said.

Thank goodness! The diversion worked.

"Well, it's a good thing I'm here, then. He's probably dying for a decent cup of coffee. And some breakfast, too."

"I'm sure he is," I agreed.

Mrs. Pervis gave a curt nod. "I'll go start the coffee right now," she said.

I let out my breath as Mrs. Pervis disappeared into the kitchen. But I knew this was only the beginning. How was I going to keep Ellie a secret from my father and Mrs. Pervis? Keeping promises to children, I was beginning to realize, was a lot harder than it seemed.

Up in my room, I finally managed to calm Ellie down by telling her that I couldn't continue to hide her if she made too much noise, and by giving her another one of my favorite dolls to play with. She promptly went into the bathroom and washed the doll's gorgeous blue-black hair, totally ruining it.

At least it wasn't Sarah, I told myself.

But aside from that, everything seemed to be going well. Or as well as could be expected under the circumstances. An hour had passed since Mrs. Pervis and my dad came home. Neither of them had called me to breakfast or come up to ask me about the Seventh Heaven field day. I was beginning to believe that maybe I could convince Ellie to go home before they found out about her.

Then I heard the downstairs phone ring. I jumped. Was it someone looking for Ellie? Then I relaxed. So the phone rang. So what? Dad gets calls all the time.

But soon after the ringing stopped, there was a knock on my door.

"Lila?" Dad said. "May I come in?"

"Just a minute!" I called sweetly. I grabbed Ellie. "Be very quiet," I warned her, "or my daddy will send you home."

"OK," she whispered as I shoved her and the doll under the bed.

"You can come in now," I said.

My dad opened the door. He seemed upset. His eyebrows were drawn together and his lips were pursed. "Mrs. McMillan is on the phone," he said. "She's calling from the Sweet Valley Airport."

"Oh?" I said, hoping he couldn't hear my heart pounding.

"She's very upset," he said, running a hand through his hair as he paced the room. "Hysterical, in fact. It seems Ellie is missing."

I covered my mouth in feigned surprise, hoping I looked convincing. "Ellie's what?" I managed to say.

My dad nodded, his eyes anxiously scanning mine. "The police have been notified, but they don't have any leads. Mrs. McMillan was wondering if you knew anything that might help locate Ellie. If you noticed anything unusual the last time you saw Ellie."

It was all I could do to keep from blurting, *She's under the bed!* "No," I said. "Nothing unusual."

My dad shook his head, defeated. "I was afraid of that," he said. His jaw clenched. "This is terrible. What would make a child like Ellie run away?" He sighed. "All I can figure is that she was kidnapped. Only the most despicable kind of person would take a child," he said. "What a horrible thing for Mrs. McMillan to have to face. I only hope that when the person who did this is caught, he or she is sent to jail for years. Years!"

I could hardly breathe, I was so scared. I couldn't tell my dad about Ellie now, even if I hadn't promised. He'd hate me!

He smiled apologetically at me. "I'm sorry if I upset you," he said. "But taking a child . . ." He stepped into the hallway. "I'll tell Mrs. McMillan that you don't have any information," he said. He left me standing in the doorway.

"What am I going to do?" I groaned, closing the door and sitting on the edge of my bed.

Ellie came crawling out from beneath the bed, her eyes wide. "Are you in trouble?" she asked.

I nodded. "I sure am," I said. "You have to go home, Ellie. The police will arrest me for kidnapping you if you don't."

I expected Ellie to immediately turn herself over to her mother, once she knew the kind of trouble I was in. But she shook her head. "I don't want to go home. My mommy doesn't love me anymore. She loves Mr. Stillman. I want to stay here with you," she said.

"But, Ellie," I pleaded.

"My mommy and Mr. Stillman are going to go away and leave me all by myself if you send me home!" she said fearfully. Then her face tightened into an angry pout. "I'll scream if you tell them I'm here," she threatened. "Then the police will arrest you."

My mouth dropped open. I couldn't believe it! The little angel from the day-care center had turned into a blackmailer. I understood why she didn't want to go home, but blackmail? It was one thing to do something because you were keeping your word to someone, but another to do it because that someone was threatening you. I suddenly wanted to tell my dad the whole truth.

But then I'd be in major trouble. Not only would I be arrested for kidnapping, but Dad would probably never speak to me again.

"Don't scream," I said. "OK? If you want to stay here, you can't scream."

Ellie closed her eyes and turned her nose up. "If I scream," she said, "the police will get you."

"That's not very nice, Ellie," I said.

"I don't care," she said. "I want an ice-cream

cone." She stomped her foot. "Right now!"

"But, Ellie," I said, "it's only nine o'clock in the morning!"

"Now!" she yelled.

I put my hand over her mouth. "Shhh," I said. "OK, OK! I'll get you an ice-cream cone."

"Chocolate," she said.

"Chocolate," I repeated.

"With sprinkles."

I rolled my eyes. Great. How was I going to get Ellie an ice-cream cone at nine in the morning without alerting Dad and Mrs. Pervis?

Richard! I suddenly remembered that Richard had a sweet tooth. He told me that he once ate a pound of chocolates someone had given him for Christmas in one sitting.

I picked up the intercom and hit Richard's button. "Yes, miss?" he said.

I forced a laugh. "Richard, this is going to sound really crazy, but I was wondering if you could do me a favor? I've got a real craving for a chocolate ice-cream cone with sprinkles, and I wanted to know if you could go get one for me."

Richard laughed. "I didn't know you had a sweet tooth, miss," he said.

I shot a withering look at Ellie. "Sometimes it flares up," I said. "I'll tell Mrs. Pervis I sent you out for aspirins, OK? Don't let her know that you're buying ice cream, whatever you do. She'll have a fit that I'm eating sweets this early in the morning."

"Will do, miss," Richard said.

Ellie looked as pleased as punch when I finished.

"I want you to read me a story," she said.

"Look, Ellie . . ." I said.

"Read me a story!" she shouted.

"OK, just make it something other than *The Cat in the Hat*, would you?"

She searched through the old children's books on my bookshelf and pulled out a story about a stuffed rabbit.

"Read it!" she commanded, snuggling close to me.

I opened the book and began to read.

I read the stuffed-rabbit story three times, and a story about a lost kitten and puppy four times, and was just about to start the fifth reading of a story about a fairy and a lost tooth, when I closed the book.

"I can't do this anymore," I said. "My throat's getting sore."

Ellie pouted for a second, then shrugged. "OK," she said. "Get me something to eat."

"But you just ate an ice-cream cone an hour ago."

"I want something to eat!" Ellie insisted, her voice rising.

"All right," I said. "What do you want?"

She tapped her finger on her chin. "Peanut butter, banana, and jelly," she said.

I grimaced. "Yuck!" I said. "Wouldn't you prefer a whole-wheat English muffin with marmalade?"

"No!" Ellie screeched. "I want peanut butter, banana, and jelly! No lumps!"

"Yes, your majesty," I said, going to the kitchen.

When I got downstairs, I tiptoed to the kitchen and checked to see if Mrs. Pervis was around. Good. The coast was clear. She'd be sure to know something was up if she saw me making something as disgusting as a peanut-butter, banana, and jelly sandwich.

Hurriedly, I slapped peanut butter on some bread and added a few slices of banana. I searched the refrigerator and cupboards for jelly, and finally found some mint jelly behind a jar of sun-dried tomatoes.

"Jelly! All right!" I said.

I smeared the green jelly on the top piece of bread and was just about to carry it upstairs, when I heard Mrs. Pervis's footsteps. Quickly, I ripped a piece of paper towel from the roll above the sink, wrapped the sandwich, and hid it under my shirt.

Mrs. Pervis started when she walked into the kitchen and saw me. "Lila, what are you doing here?" she asked.

"I, um, just wanted to get a drink," I said.

She looked confused. "You could have rung me," she said.

I shrugged. "I didn't want to bother you."

She reached out and touched my forehead. "Are

you feeling all right?" she asked. "Maybe that headache was caused by a fever."

"I'm fine," I said. "Got to go!"

I started from the kitchen.

"Lila?" Mrs. Pervis said.

"Yes?"

"What about your drink?"

I laughed nervously. "Oh, right," I said. I shrugged. "I guess I'm not that thirsty after all."

I felt her eyes on me as I hurried back upstairs. "Where's my sandwich?" Ellie demanded as soon as I got inside the room.

"It's right here," I said, pulling the sandwich from underneath my shirt. "Here!" I handed Ellie the sandwich.

Ellie looked at it this way and that. Then she made a face. "What's that?" she said, pointing to the mint jelly.

I flung up my hands in exasperation. "It's jelly," I said. "You told me you wanted jelly, didn't you?"

Ellie put the sandwich down. "Jelly's purple, not green," she said.

"It's mint jelly," I explained. "Try it, it's good."

"Jelly's purple!" she insisted.

"Not all jelly's purple, Ellie," I said.

"Purple!" she screamed.

"Shh," I said.

"Purple, purple, purple. Get me purple jelly!"

"Be quiet!" I hissed. "We don't have purple jelly."

"Tell Richard to get me some!"

I crossed my arms. Enough was enough. "I am not sending Richard out to get purple jelly."

"Tell Richard!" Ellie said, her face turning red.

"No!"

The next thing I knew Ellie opened her mouth, and out came a screech that was somewhere between fingernails on a blackboard and a fighting cat.

"All right!" I said. "I'll send Richard to get purple jelly. Just be quiet."

But it was too late. Just then my father knocked on the door and asked me what all the racket was.

I ran to the door and peeked out. "Sorry, Daddy," I said. "I was just listening to a new heavy-metal band."

My father rolled his eyes. "Please keep it down," he said. "I can hardly hear myself think."

"Sure," I said, closing the door.

I glared at Ellie. "Thanks a lot," I said.

Ellie shrugged. "You should have gotten me the right kind of jelly."

What I should have done, I thought, was called the baby-sitter right away, while I still had the chance. Because right now I was wishing I had never laid eyes on Ellie McMillan.

Eleven

"There has to be something we can do," Maria said. She was sitting on the flowered couch in the den later that morning. "We can't just let Ellie ruin Lila's life!"

"Maybe we can bribe Ellie with some new toys," Mandy suggested.

Maria sat up. "Yeah," she said. "Kids will do practically anything for a new toy."

"I don't know," Elizabeth said, shaking her head. "That's like giving Ellie a reward for being rotten."

I sighed. "Elizabeth's right," I said. "If we promise Ellie new toys now to make her do what she's supposed to do, she might start misbehaving just so she can get things."

"What a mess," Mandy said, taking off the fedora she was wearing and resting it on her lap. "I guess we can strike that idea."

It was almost noon, and the entire Unicorn Club was sitting in the den, eating pretzels and drinking cranberry-juice spritzers, trying to figure out what to do about Ellie. We'd been there for nearly an hour. Jessica and Ellen had decided they needed some help coming up with a solution to my problem, so they told the rest of the Unicorns about Ellie's running away. At first I was really angry. Here I was going crazy trying to keep my promise to Ellie, and they broke their promise to me not to tell anyone the minute the going got rough.

But my anger faded pretty fast when I realized that eight heads are definitely better than three— especially when those three had been unable to come up with a solution for fifteen hours.

Besides, it made me feel really good that the Unicorns cared about me like that. I mean, they had to miss a major part of the field day to come here. Still, I had begun to wonder if there was anything they could do to help.

"Maybe we can just tell her that there's a present waiting for her at home," Ellen suggested, biting a pretzel stick.

"What, lie to her?" I said. "After all I've been through? And anyway, that's not fair."

Jessica frowned. "Well, Ellie hasn't been acting very fair to you, has she?"

I sighed. "No," I said, "but she's only a little girl.

And she's scared. She thinks her mother doesn't love her anymore. I can't let her think I don't love her, either. Lying to her would be as bad as breaking a promise."

"Lila's right," Evie said. "I'm sure Ellie doesn't really understand how serious this is."

I stared at my fingers. "I guess there's nothing I can do," I said. "I'll just have to wait until the police come and take me away in handcuffs."

Elizabeth put her arm around my shoulders. "We're Unicorns, remember?" she said. "We don't give up that easily."

"Believe me," I said, "it hasn't been easy."

"I say we go up to your room and try to figure out how to get Ellie home," Elizabeth said.

"It won't help," I said.

"It can't hurt," Elizabeth countered.

I shrugged. "OK, let's give it one more try," I said.

"That's the spirit," Elizabeth said, and we all headed for my room.

Ellie was sitting on my bed playing with the ruined black-haired doll when we walked into the room.

"Where were you?" she demanded, her eyes big with anxiety. "I thought you were going away, like Mommy."

"I wouldn't leave you, Ellie," I said, stroking her hair.

"I hate Mommy!" Ellie said, the fear in her eyes turning to anger.

The Unicorns exchanged glances, then looked at me.

"Whoa!" Maria said out of the side of her mouth. "Is this the same Ellie we took care of at the day-care center? That sweet little kid?"

I sighed. "The very same," I said.

Jessica and Elizabeth went and sat down near Ellie. Then the rest of the Unicorns joined them in a circle.

"What are you playing?" Mandy asked.

Ellie stared at her feet and shyly twisted her body back and forth. "Nothing," she said.

"Who's this?" Mandy asked, touching the doll's ruined hair.

"It's Lila's doll," Ellie murmured.

"Are you pretending to be the doll's mommy?" Mandy asked.

Ellie suddenly lost her shyness and glared at Mandy. "It's Lila's doll," she snapped. "Lila's her mommy!"

Mandy's head jerked back. "Wow!" she said. "She's changed!"

"I am not changed!" Ellie shouted. "Only babies get changed. I don't wear diapers!"

Mandy sighed. "I give up," she said.

Elizabeth shrugged. "No one said it was going to be easy."

Maria moved closer to Ellie. "So, Ellie, have you been having fun with Lila?" she asked.

Ellie nodded. "Yes," she said.

"That's because you love Lila, right?"

Ellie plucked a loose hair from the doll's head. "Yes," she answered cautiously.

The other Unicorns leaned closer. I leaned closer. Maybe Maria was onto something here.

"When somebody loves someone," Maria said, "they don't do anything to hurt them, do they?"

Ellie shook her head. "No," she said.

Maria looked at the group knowingly and nodded. "It's hurting Lila that you won't go home," she said. "Lila can get in big trouble."

Ellie's brow furrowed as she thought about what Maria had said.

Maria smiled triumphantly at the group.

"I won't tell anyone on Lila if she doesn't tell on me," Ellie said finally.

"But, Ellie," Mary said, "once they find you, Lila will be in big, big trouble."

"They won't find me"—Ellie looked around the room suspiciously—"unless you tell."

"Mr. Fowler or Mrs. Pervis will discover you're here sooner or later," Ellen said in her usual blunt way.

"No they won't!" Ellie said, her face growing red.

"Yes they will," Ellen insisted.

"No!" Ellie said.

"Be quiet!" Jessica said to Ellen. "Can't you see you're upsetting her?"

It was true. Ellie looked as though she were about to explode.

"It's OK, Ellie," I said, trying to calm her down.

"No one will find out you're here. I promised you that already."

"They'll tell!" she said, pointing to the other Unicorns.

"No they won't," I assured her. "They're my friends, and they promised they won't tell."

Ellie began to breathe hard, as if she was going to throw a tantrum any minute.

"If only I hadn't promised I wouldn't tell where she is," I whispered. "I can't break my word to her. But I know keeping her a secret is the wrong thing to do. I don't even know Mrs. McMillan's side of the story."

Elizabeth had been sitting quietly in the circle, thinking. Suddenly, she smiled. "Lila," she said, pulling me into a corner of the room.

"I'm going to scream . . ." Ellie threatened in a low voice.

"I have to calm Ellie," I said to Elizabeth, trying to pull away.

Elizabeth shook her head. "No you don't," she said.

"But she'll scream," I said, glancing anxiously at Ellie, whose mouth was beginning to open.

"Exactly," Elizabeth said, grinning.

I looked at her as if she were crazy. "Huh?"

Elizabeth glanced at the rest of the group, then back at me. "You don't have to tell anyone where Ellie is," she said softly. "Let Ellie tell where Ellie is."

The Unicorns smiled at each other as they passed

Elizabeth's idea along in a whisper so Ellie wouldn't hear. It took me a minute or two to understand, but when I did, I gave Elizabeth a thumbs-up signal and a grin. "You're a genius!" I said.

Elizabeth pretended to polish her nails on her shirt. "All in a day's work," she said.

Jessica picked up a pillow and threw it at her.

Meanwhile, Ellie was working herself up to a tantrum, annoyed that no one was paying attention to her threats. "I'm going to scream," she said, looking first at me and then at all the other Unicorns. "I'm going to count to three and scream."

We all just watched her, smiling. "Go ahead," I said. Ellie's eyebrows drew together angrily. She opened her mouth and let out an earth-shattering scream. Then she smiled triumphantly at me, expecting me to run to her and beg her to stop.

"So," I said, nonchalantly turning to Jessica, "do you think we'll be out of here in time to make the field-day barbecue?"

Ellie's face grew red. She opened her mouth and screamed even louder.

Evie blocked her ears. "I don't want her to ruin my perfect-pitch hearing," she said with a grin.

Elizabeth nodded. "Naturally," she said.

Now Ellie was really mad. She dropped to the floor and began to scream even louder, kicking and pounding the floor at the same time.

"She's got strong lungs for a little girl," Maria said over the racket.

I nodded. "Maybe she'll be an Olympic swimmer when she gets older," I said.

Ellie raised the pitch of her scream to a deafening screech. Just as she did, the door to my room flew open. Dad and Mrs. Pervis were standing in the doorway.

"What's going on?" Dad demanded. Then he and Mrs. Pervis caught sight of Ellie.

Mrs. Pervis gasped. My dad's eyes practically bulged out of his head.

"Lila Fowler," he said sternly, "you have some very serious explaining to do."

Twelve

The doorbell rang just before one o'clock. "It's Mrs. McMillan," Mrs. Pervis announced.

I looked anxiously at the other Unicorns. They had stayed to wait for Mrs. McMillan with me.

"Don't worry," Jessica said, squeezing my hand. "It'll be all right."

I took a deep breath. "I hope so," I said. According to Mrs. Pervis, Mrs. McMillan had been relieved when Dad told her Ellie was here, but then she had gotten very angry at me.

Mrs. McMillan walked into the room and immediately ran to Ellie, who was contentedly sitting on my dad's lap, listening to a story about a fairy princess.

"Ellie!" Mrs. McMillan said. "Oh, sweetheart, I was so worried!"

"Mommy!" Ellie squealed, squirming off my dad's lap to run to her mother.

The two hugged each other tight. Then Mrs. McMillan put Ellie down. "Honey, I have to talk to Lila for just a minute. Will you please go with Mrs. Pervis?" Ellie nodded, and Mrs. Pervis took her to the kitchen.

Mrs. McMillan turned toward me. The look on her face changed from a smile to complete outrage.

"I don't understand how you could have done such a thing," she said to me. "You must have known how upset I'd be. Why didn't you tell anyone Ellie was here?"

I took a deep breath, drawing courage from the other Unicorns, and stepped toward Mrs. McMillan. "I'm really sorry about making you worry so much, Mrs. McMillan," I said. "But Ellie overheard you and Mr. Stillman talking about going away together and leaving her behind."

"What?" Mrs. McMillan said. She looked shocked. "Do you really think I would do something like that?"

I faced her squarely. "Not really," I said. "But you have been paying a lot more attention to Mr. Stillman than to Ellie lately. Then I remembered what you told me about Mr. Stillman not wanting children and how he wanted to travel, and I thought it was at least possible that you were planning to leave Ellie in a foster home so you could go with him. Ellie said you told Mr. Stillman you had to find someone to take care of her before you left with him."

Mrs. McMillan covered her mouth with her hand. Her eyes grew wide. "Oh, no!" she said. "Now I understand! Ellie did hear me making plans to go away with Gerard, but we were making plans for our honeymoon. Gerard and I are getting married!"

"Married?" I said.

"Wow!" Ellen said. "How romantic!"

"Congratulations," the other Unicorns said.

I didn't know what to say. "Th-th-that's wonderful," I stuttered. "Um, congratulations."

"Thank you," Mrs. McMillan said.

Relief flooded through me as Mrs. McMillan went to find Ellie. Things were going to be okay.

"I didn't know my poor little girl was feeling so lost!" Mrs. McMillan was saying as the two returned. She enfolded Ellie in her arms and covered her face with kisses. "I love you more than anyone in the whole world," she told Ellie. "And I would never leave you. Not for anyone or anything."

"But you love Mr. Stillman," Ellie said, searching her mother's face.

Mrs. McMillan cupped Ellie's face in her hands. "Yes, I do," she said. "But no one can ever take your place in my heart, Ellie. If Gerard didn't love you, too, I wouldn't marry him."

"You wouldn't?" Ellie said, her eyes wide.

Mrs. McMillan smiled. "No, I wouldn't," she said, nuzzling Ellie's neck. "But he loves you like crazy. As a matter of fact, I think you're one of the main reasons he asked me to marry him so quickly. He thinks you're a very special little girl." She hugged Ellie tightly. "And so do I."

Ellie grinned. Then she looked shyly at me. "I'm sorry for being bad, Lila," she said.

I smiled at her. "You weren't bad, Ellie," I said, "just upset."

"But you didn't tell on me," Ellie said.

"No," I agreed. "I didn't tell."

Mrs. McMillan looked questioningly at me.

"That's why I couldn't tell you Ellie was here, even when I began to think I should," I explained. "I promised Ellie I wouldn't tell anyone where she was. I couldn't break my promise to her. If something was really wrong between you and her, I didn't want her to lose her faith in me."

Mrs. McMillan looked at me with a grim expression. "Sometimes, as a matter of safety, a promise should be broken. And this was probably one of those times. You caused me and my baby-sitter unimaginable grief, Lila." Her face softened. "But I know you were trying to do what was best. And Ellie's safe and sound."

She took a deep breath. "I had no idea Ellie was so troubled about Gerard," she said. She hugged Ellie tightly again. Then she smiled at me.

"I want to thank you for being such a loyal friend to Ellie, Lila, and for taking care of her," she said. "I know you would rather have been off at the Seventh Heaven Weekend with your friends."

I looked from one Unicorn to the other, then at Mrs. McMillan and Ellie. "Maybe it isn't exactly seventh heaven," I said, "but all my friends are here."

"Where else would we be when a sister Unicorn is in trouble?" Ellen said.

Jessica grinned. "I know where else," she said. "How about the Seventh Heaven Weekend? Isn't it about time we showed our faces at some of the field-day events?"

Maria put an arm around Jessica's shoulders. "I'm with you," she said.

The Unicorns began to gather their things together.

"Before you go, girls," Mrs. McMillan said, "I want to thank all of you for your help this weekend. And invite you to my wedding."

"Great!" Mandy said. "You know, there's this fantastic nineteen-twenties dress at The Attic that would be just perfect for a wedding."

"For me?" Mrs. McMillan said.

Mandy smiled. "It's gorgeous. Yellow satin, very sleek. That is, unless you wanted to buy something new."

Mrs. McMillan grinned. "To tell you the truth, Mandy, I think it was that fantastic outfit you picked for our first date that started everything," she said. "You can pick my clothes for me anytime."

Everyone laughed.

Jessica looked at the Unicorns. "I guess it's time to head out," she said.

"Right," Elizabeth said, "to the Seventh Heaven field day."

Evie sighed. "To violin practice."

Elizabeth looked confused. "Oh, did I forget to tell you?" she said. "The Seventh Heaven contests are judged by kids in other grades—it makes the judging impartial. That's why Mary's with us. She's judging the watermelon-eating contest."

Evie looked at Mary, who shrugged. "It's better than being in the contest," Mary said.

"Anyway," Elizabeth continued, "they've got a couple of other eighth graders judging the hip-hop contest, and they need someone to act as a tie breaker." She grinned at the adults. "Obviously, a grown-up won't do."

"So?" Evie said.

"So," Elizabeth explained, "I volunteered you. I told Mr. Clark that with your musical background, you had a great sense of rhythm. Naturally, you're invited to spend the day."

"All right!" Evie said, smiling.

Elizabeth grinned.

The Unicorns exchanged glances. "Are we ready?" Maria asked.

"Ready," everyone said.

The Unicorns, Ellie, and Mrs. McMillan started for the door. I held back.

"Aren't you coming?" Mary asked.

"I'll meet you there," I said, glancing at my father. "I think my dad and I need to talk."

*   *   *

The house was very quiet after everyone left, but it didn't feel lonely. Dad was there. Besides, after the fiasco with Ellie, the quiet was kind of nice.

I sat down on the brocade couch across from my father. "I just wanted to tell you I'm sorry for lying to you about Ellie's being here," I told him. I kept my gaze focused on my lap. I felt bad.

Dad came over and sat beside me. His eyebrows were drawn together, the way they were when something was bothering him. "I should be apologizing to you," he said.

I looked up, confused. "What?" I said.

"I blame myself for what happened," Dad explained. He took a deep breath and let it out again. "I'm gone too much. If I'd been home, this wouldn't have gone so far."

I wanted to tell him that he shouldn't blame himself, but deep down, I knew what he had said was true. We both had been wrong. As much as I hated to give Mrs. Riteman credit for being right, I realized that parenting was a lot harder than it looked. Children and parents needed to be together. It was hard enough that my dad was raising me without a mother. Being gone as often as he was made it almost impossible.

"You are gone an awful lot, Dad," I said. "Sometimes I get really lonely. Sometimes I feel like I don't have a mother or a father."

Dad sighed and nodded slowly.

"I know," he said. "I should have realized I was leaving you alone too much. It's just that you seem so mature and independent. I forget sometimes that you're still a little girl." He put an arm around my shoulder and pulled me close. "I'll make more of an effort to be here for you from now on," he said. "And I won't break any more promises."

"Thanks, Dad," I said. "I know how hard it can be to keep promises to children." I flipped my hair over my shoulders. "I've learned to appreciate some of the difficulties of being a parent this past weekend."

Dad smiled. I guess he thought that my observation was pretty mature. "I've learned to appreciate some of the difficulties of being a daughter, too," he said, giving me a hug.

Thirteen

"So where should we start?" my dad asked.

It was Sunday afternoon. The potluck supper was five hours away, and Dad seemed to know less about what to do in a kitchen than I did. But we'd decided to make something with our very own hands to take to the potluck supper. It would give us some time together. And it would be fun.

At least, that's what I had thought yesterday. But now I was beginning to think we'd bitten off more than we could chew. I shrugged. "Maybe we should have asked Mrs. Pervis to help us," I said.

My father waved the suggestion off. "It's Mrs. Pervis's day off. Besides, we can do this. We're a team, right?"

I shrugged. "Right," I said, tying an apron around my waist. Even if the casserole turned out lousy, I was spending some time with my dad. That was what was important. I looked at the recipe card on the counter. We'd chosen a crab and rice casserole from Mrs. Pervis's recipe file.

"Let's see," I said. "According to this, first we have to cook the rice."

He nodded. "OK," he said, picking up the box of rice. Luckily, Mrs. Pervis had assembled all the ingredients for us beforehand, so we wouldn't have to search for everything. "How much rice do we need?"

"It says three cups of cooked rice makes six servings," I told him. "But Mrs. Pervis said we should double the recipe."

"OK," Dad said, "so we need six cups of cooked rice." I nodded. Dad scratched his forehead, reading the cooking instructions on the rice box.

"Hmm," he said. "For three cups of cooked rice you need two cups of water and one cup of rice. So for six cups of rice, we need four cups of water and two cups of rice."

"Sounds good," I said.

Dad looked confused.

"What's the matter?" I asked.

Dad smiled uncertainly. "What size cup should we use?" he asked. "A mug or a teacup?"

I giggled. Even I knew what a cup in a recipe was. I guess some of my home-economics class had sunk in after all.

"We need a measuring cup," I told him, looking through the cupboards until I found one. "Like this!" I said, showing him the cup. He grinned.

"Thank goodness we're doing this together," he said, choosing a tiny copper saucepan from among the pans hanging above the maple work island in the kitchen.

"I think that's going to be too small," I said. I picked out a much larger pan. "You'd be surprised how things expand when they're cooked," I explained, remembering the popcorn.

"Good thinking," Dad said, patting me on the shoulder.

We put the water in the saucepan and waited for it to boil, as the box said. Then we added the rice.

"OK, now," Dad said, reading the recipe. "We need to make a cream sauce."

I nodded. "Everything's here," I said, pointing to the butter, flour, and milk. "The recipe says to melt the butter."

Dad stuck a knife in it. "Does that seem melted to you?" he asked.

I grinned. "Didn't you ever cook anything?" I asked.

He shrugged. "Marshmallows over a campfire," he said. "But that was years ago."

I laughed. "We have to melt the butter in a pan on the stove," I said. "It has to be liquid."

Dad looked at me in surprise. "How do you know that?"

I tossed my hair over my shoulders. "Just smart, I guess," I said.

Dad grinned. "I guess," he said.

We both laughed.

I stuck six tablespoons of butter in the saucepan and turned up the heat. "See?" I said smugly as the butter began to melt. Then I felt my smile disappearing. The butter was turning brown! Was it supposed to turn brown?

Before I could check the recipe, smoke began to pour out of the pan. "Take it off the stove!" I yelled to my father.

He grabbed the pan before the smoke alarm went off. "Now what?" he said.

"Well," I said, taking down another pan. "If at first you don't succeed—"

"Try, try again," Dad finished.

"This time on lower heat," I said.

That worked. Soon the butter was melted and golden. We added flour to it, and then milk, salt, and pepper. "It says to stir constantly until the mixture thickens," I said, looking at the recipe.

Dad nodded and began to stir the mixture. At first nothing happened. Then, suddenly, the mixture began to thicken to a real cream sauce. It was amazing!

Once the rice and the cream sauce were ready, we mixed the sauce, rice, and crab together, and spread it in a buttered casserole dish. We added buttered bread crumbs to the top, then put it into the oven to bake. An hour later, we had a beautiful crab and rice casserole.

"Wow!" I said when Dad pulled it out of the oven.

"It looks as good as one of Mrs. Pervis's casseroles!"

Dad beamed. "I never knew cooking could be so much fun," he said, looking proudly at the casserole and then at me. "I'm glad we decided to do this."

"Me, too," I said, smiling. I felt happier than I'd felt in a long time.

When Dad and I arrived later that evening, the school cafeteria was completely transformed. Along one wall was a smorgasbord of Sterno-heated dishes and fancy desserts. A bunch of the tables had been placed together and covered with white tablecloths with gold trim. In the center of all the food was a paper angel with a gold harp.

"Seventh heaven," Dad said with a smile.

I grinned. "You got it!" I said.

The rest of the seventh-grade Unicorns—except for Mandy and her mom—were already there, sitting with their parents at a long table near the front of the room.

I waved.

"I saved you some seats!" Jessica called to me before Dad and I went up to the buffet. Mandy and her mom were at the buffet table when I proudly placed the crab and rice casserole in one of the Sterno pans.

"What's that?" Mandy asked.

"Crab and rice casserole," I said. "Dad and I made it ourselves." I grinned at my dad.

Mrs. Miller smiled. "I love seafood," she said, taking a big spoonful of the casserole.

"Me, too," Mandy said.

Dad and I took some of our casserole. I added some salad, and Dad tried a bit of Mrs. Wakefield's shepherd's pie. Then we went over to the Unicorn table. There were two empty seats beside Jessica, and two more on the other side of the table beside Ellen.

"Sit here," Jessica said, patting the seat beside her.

"Thanks," I said. I sat next to Jessica. My dad's seat was between mine and Mrs. Riteman's. Ellen was sitting across from her mother.

"You have to try the pot roast," Ellen said, pointing out the beef, carrots, and potatoes on her plate. "My mom makes the best."

I smiled smugly. "And you have to try the crab and rice casserole," I told her, pointing to my dish. "My dad and I spent all afternoon making it."

"You and your dad?" Ellen exclaimed, amazed.

"That's what I hear," Mandy chimed in, returning from the buffet table with her mother. "And it smells delicious."

I couldn't help grinning. I was having a great time. Across the table, Mrs. Riteman was bending Dad's ear, but he didn't seem to mind. He was smiling and nodding at whatever Mrs. Riteman was saying to him. Even Mrs. Riteman looked as though she was in a good mood. I didn't think I'd ever seen her smile so much.

Jessica nudged Elizabeth. "Let's go get some dessert," she said.

"Are you crazy?" Elizabeth said. "I couldn't eat another bite!"

"But you haven't had any of my mom's famous cherry cheesecake," Maria protested.

"Or my mom's chocolate cake," Mandy added, grinning at Mrs. Miller.

"That settles it," Jessica said. "I'm going up there."

"Me, too," Maria said.

A few minutes later, Elizabeth, Jessica, Mandy, Maria, Ellen, and I were up at the buffet table, sampling the desserts.

"Scrumptious!" Jessica said, testing the chocolate cake.

"Ditto for the cheesecake," Elizabeth added. Apparently, she'd found some room in her stomach. We carried our plates back to the table.

"So who signed up to work on the all-school play?" Mandy asked. "I know Evie did, because she's working on the costumes with me."

Jessica, Ellen, and Maria all began to giggle. Maria explained, "We all got acting parts, and some of us are even interested in the acting." She glared at Jessica and Ellen.

"Can I help it if I'm a natural actress?" Jessica said.

I rolled my eyes. If Jessica wasn't figuring out how to get on TV or in a movie, she wasn't interested in acting—period. But this year's all-school play featured something Jessica cared about even more than getting in the limelight: boys!

Is romance in the air on the set of the all-school play? Find out in THE UNICORN CLUB #5: **Unicorns In Love.**

SIGN UP FOR THE SWEET VALLEY HIGH® FAN CLUB!

Hey, girls! Get all the gossip on Sweet Valley High's® most popular teenagers when you join our fantastic Fan Club! As a member, you'll get all of this really cool stuff:

- Membership Card with your own personal Fan Club ID number
- A Sweet Valley High® Secret Treasure Box
- Sweet Valley High® Stationery
- Official Fan Club Pencil (for secret note writing!)
- Three Bookmarks
- A "Members Only" Door Hanger
- Two Skeins of J. & P. Coats® Embroidery Floss with flower barrette instruction leaflet
- Two editions of *The Oracle* newsletter
- Plus exclusive Sweet Valley High® product offers, special savings, contests, and much more!

Be the first to find out what Jessica & Elizabeth Wakefield are up to by joining the Sweet Valley High® Fan Club for the one-year membership fee of only $6.25 each for U.S. residents, $8.25 for Canadian residents (U.S. currency). Includes shipping & handling.

Send a check or money order (do not send cash) made payable to "Sweet Valley High® Fan Club" along with this form to:

SWEET VALLEY HIGH® FAN CLUB, BOX 3919-B, SCHAUMBURG, IL 60168-3919

NAME_____
(Please print clearly)

ADDRESS_____

CITY_____ STATE _____ ZIP_____
(Required)

AGE_____ BIRTHDAY_____ /_____ /_____

Offer good while supplies last. Allow 6-8 weeks after check clearance for delivery. Addresses without ZIP codes cannot be honored. Offer good in USA & Canada only. Void where prohibited by law.
©1993 by Francine Pascal   LCI-1383-123